HEATHER BOYD

BESTSELLING AUTHOR

A GENTLEMAN'S VOW

SAINTS AND SINNERS SERIES

BOOK 1: THE DUKE AND I
BOOK 2: A GENTLEMAN'S VOW
BOOK 3: AN EARL OF HER OWN
BOOK 4: THE LADY TAMED

The characters and events portrayed in this book are fictitious. Any similarity to real persons, living or dead, is purely coincidental and not intended by the author.

A GENTLEMAN'S VOW
Copyright © 2018 by Heather Boyd
Edited by Kelli Collins

Cover Design and Formatting by Heather Boyd

Dedication

———•———

For my rogues, Lachlan and Finn. Thanks for the hugs, love and silliness. You make me so proud to be your mum. (Don't worry, you only need to read this one page. Close the book now and back away.)

And for my favorite rogue John, my best friend for so many years. Only you make me laugh like no one can. Thanks for always being there for me.

xoxo

Chapter One

---·---

April 1st 1819

A reputation for having an easy disposition and no other responsibilities was a curse to be borne at a country gathering. Gideon navigated the stifling alehouse, sweat trickling down his spine as he carried two drinks through the chattering crowd of mourners. Determined not to spill one single drop, which would mean starting over, he concentrated on his errand and ignored the assessing glances thrown his way.

The late Mr. Grieves had been well liked and it seemed everyone in the district had come to mourn together in the village tavern. *Everyone*, unfortunately, included a few too many widows, or wives with daughters of marriageable age in want of a husband.

Being the sole bachelor in a crowd was an uncomfortable experience at Gideon's age.

"There you are, madam," he murmured to Mrs. Hawthorne as he passed over the punch, and then glanced around for young Miss Natalia Hawthorne. He didn't immediately see her, so he held on to her glass.

Mrs. Hawthorne craned her neck to look beyond him. "What became of my husband, Mr. Whitfield?"

Gideon glanced over his shoulder in surprise. Mr. Hawthorne, carrying two tankards of ale, had vanished. Gideon suppressed a groan. Hawthorne must have slipped outside instead of returning to his wife. "I'm sure he'll be along any moment."

Gideon had no choice but to remain in the oppressive heat with Mrs. Hawthorne, at least until Miss Hawthorne returned to take her cup of punch. He studied the crowd again, wondering where the girl had gone to this time. Natalia Hawthorne tended to disappear from her mother's side with alarming frequency.

Mrs. Hawthorne's lips pinched tightly together and he averted his eyes. She would, of course, be displeased that her husband had quit the very crowded tavern without seeing to his family's comfort. Wives were said to be highly combative, not that he'd know from personal experience. He'd never married. But he'd overheard the odd argument, whispered complaints and such, from male acquaintances. They were never allowed a moment's peace. Still, today, Mr. Hawthorne was very much in the wrong.

He glanced around for the daughter discreetly once more. He should never have made that foolish promise to watch over Natalia Hawthorne.

He leaned closer to Mrs. Hawthorne. "Where has she gone?"

Mrs. Hawthorne patted his arm. "She's sitting with Mrs. Grieves, right behind you."

"Ah, good." He glanced over his shoulder and, sure enough, the girl—or woman, he should say now, because she'd been out for two years—was speaking earnestly to the newly made widow who appeared to be crying yet again.

"You are so kind to worry," Mrs. Hawthorne said. "It means so much to our family that you concern yourself when you have no obligation to us."

Gideon was not related to the Hawthornes, but they were friends of *his* absent friends, and therefore important. He had made an attempt to ensure the Hawthorne ladies would not expire from thirst in this dreadful heat. What more could a bachelor be expected to do?

Nothing. He glanced at the glass of punch

in his hand with a wry smile, wishing it were the ale Mr. Hawthorne had taken with him.

"You must long to rejoin the gentlemen outside," Mrs. Hawthorne murmured, lips lifting in a half smile. The act of smiling, forgetting her husband's neglect, transformed her face, making her appear a jolly sort of woman. He recalled that she'd once been that way all the time. At least, at the start of her marriage she had been.

"Not at all," he murmured.

Her smile grew. "My dear Mr. Whitfield, what a terrible liar you are."

"No. No. I speak nothing but the truth," he promised. "There is nowhere I'd rather be."

Mrs. Hawthorne laughed softly. "You, sir, are the very best companion when a woman's spirits are low. Thank you for keeping me company."

"Happy to be of service," he promised.

"Oh, are you still here?" Natalia Hawthorne appeared at his side, hand extending to take the cup of punch intended for her, displeasure turning down her lips. "Thank you."

He handed over the glass without a word.

Miss Hawthorne stared at him over the rim of her cup, eyes narrowing. "You don't have to linger today."

"You might be right." He grinned. "I am happy to observe that all the scoundrels seem to have avoided the wake."

"That is nothing to be happy about," Miss Hawthorne grumbled quietly. "I can't very well reform a rake if none of them show up to start with."

He nodded solicitously. Reforming a rake was all Miss Hawthorne ever talked about. "Finding a husband is never easy, I hear."

"Indeed you are correct," Mrs. Hawthorne murmured. "The best spouses are often the most difficult to catch."

"So everyone tells me." Gideon wasn't quite sure what sort of character deserved to catch Miss Hawthorne, but thought he'd better have patience to spare. The woman spoke her mind and admired younger gentlemen quite openly.

Why had Lady Jessica Westfall, the daughter of his best friend, the Duke of Stapleton, begged him to help Natalia secure a husband while she was away in London enjoying her first season? Had it been purely to torture him from afar?

Most likely—although she probably didn't see it that way.

Mrs. Hawthorne craned her neck to look about the room again. "I have not seen Mrs. Napier's sister yet. I was sure Mrs. Beck would make an appearance."

Gideon frowned. "Who?"

Mrs. Hawthorne clucked her tongue. "Mrs.

Napier's widowed sister has come to live with her at last. I told you all about it last week when you called. Such a tragedy to lose a husband at such a young age, and she has two sons in need of a father's steadying influence, too."

"Oh, yes." Napier had his hands full, and Gideon did remember some of the discussion, now he thought about the matter, but he hardly knew those involved to feel the same level of concern as Mrs. Hawthorne apparently did. He held out his hand for her empty glass. "So very sad. If you would excuse me?"

"Yes, yes. You go off, but of course we must stay for poor Mrs. Grieves' sake."

He accepted Miss Hawthorne's empty glass too, eagerly making a move toward the refreshment table, and the doorway that led to freedom. Unfortunately, he ran headlong into Mrs. Napier before he achieved his goal.

"Mr. Whitfield!" she exclaimed excitedly.

"Madam." He nodded politely to the matron, but wasn't truly interested in beginning a conversation. He glanced toward the door with longing—and his heart skipped a beat at the glimpse of a well-formed figure blocking his path. For a moment, hope bloomed in his chest. Yet the small woman, so pale she almost appeared translucent with the sunlight shining behind her, was indeed a stranger to him.

The village was not so large that new faces

were not instantly the center of attention. This woman was ten times more handsome than past newcomers, and her confident smile hinted she knew she was attractive.

"Mr. Whitfield, may I introduce my sister, Mrs. Alice Beck, formerly of Bath," Mrs. Napier murmured at his side.

For a moment, he was frustrated his escape was yet again delayed, but then he recovered his manners and offered a short bow. "A pleasure to make your acquaintance."

"And you, sir," Mrs. Beck said softly. "I have heard so much about you since my arrival."

He laughed, but he felt nerves jumping inside him. "All good things, I trust."

"The very best." She smiled and a charming pair of dimples graced her cheeks. "My brother-in-law was telling me over breakfast that your interest in botany is known all the way to London."

"I doubt that far, but I am a member of the Royal Horticultural Society. Do you have an interest in the subject?"

Mrs. Beck eased closer. "In many things, sir. I should dearly love to see the specimens you grow. I hear too that you have an astonishing array of greenhouses."

"Indeed I do, but far less than the Duke of Stapleton's estate boasts."

She beamed at him, flashing those dimples

yet again. "I should dearly love to bring my sons, if you can bear the noise of two boys under the age of ten asking a thousand questions of you."

Mrs. Napier edged closer, and Gideon felt himself hemmed in completely. "Mr. Whitfield has the patience of a saint when it comes to children."

Mrs. Beck smiled. "Do you have family?"

"No, none."

Mrs. Napier's smile widened. "None of his own, but he is closely acquainted with the Duke of Stapleton and his children, which I've written to you about before, I am sure."

"Yes, I remember something to that effect."

Gideon did not like it when people remarked on his friendship with the duke. He rarely spoke of the family to others. "The duke's children are fully grown," he told Mrs. Beck, to be sure there were no misunderstandings about the Westfall *children's* ages.

Mrs. Beck nodded. "Do they live close?"

"The Westfalls? Goodness, no." Gideon shuffled his feet a little and fought the urge to loosen his neck cloth. "Each has moved away years ago."

"Have you any news about the success of Lady Jessica's London season?" Mrs. Napier asked.

He shook his head. "I've not received news

of a wedding yet."

But he'd been expecting a letter from someone in the family any day now. Lady Jessica Westfall was sure to win hearts wherever she went.

Mrs. Beck pressed her hand to her brow suddenly. "It is so very warm inside, isn't it?"

"Indeed, it is. I was just on my way out for that reason. There were a few ladies outside earlier, where it is cooler. I saw chairs if you'd like to sit in the shade." Escorting Mrs. Beck and Mrs. Napier to them would help him escape faster, too.

Mrs. Beck beamed but Mrs. Napier declined to accompany him, although she promised to follow.

Left with only Mrs. Beck, Gideon stood uncertainly. He'd maneuvered himself into yet another situation where he had to play escort. Would he ever learn to bite his tongue?

"I would be very grateful for your company, sir," Mrs. Beck murmured.

Without any other choice, he nodded. "Very well."

He escorted Mrs. Beck to sit in a chair in the shade, but remained on his feet. "Better?"

"Indeed." Mrs. Beck beamed her dimples at him again and opened a delicate fan. She fluttered it before her face, but her eyes were trained on his. "I do appreciate your assistance today. Coming to live in a new place is not easy. My sister wants me to feel at home here but such occasions bring back so many unpleasant memories."

"Ah, yes," he murmured. *Widowed.* He would measure his words carefully unless he wanted to be responsible for a bout of tears. "How long ago did your husband pass away?"

"Well over a year now." She glanced around, lips turning down. "We lived with his brother and his wife for a time, and then my sister sent for me. It is better to live in a place that holds no memories of him."

He smiled quickly. "I do understand."

She turned back to him quickly. "You've lost someone you love, too?"

"No. I never married." He shook his head. "However, a good friend of mine was widowed years ago and it took a long time for him to recover from the loss. He only recently remarried and is very happy now."

"Then there is hope for me," she said, and then sighed.

"I'm sure there is," he promised. A woman like Mrs. Beck, so pretty, so obviously in need of support for her children, would not be overlooked. She would be swooped up soon by anyone who could afford her upkeep.

Mrs. Beck leaned forward slightly. "Would that I had your confidence, but a woman's security is a fickle thing. So much that happens is beyond our control."

Gideon looked up when he heard someone calling his name urgently.

Natalia Hawthorne burst outside, eyes wide as she looked around. Mrs. Napier hovered behind her.

"Mr. Whitfield, there you are," Miss Hawthorne chided as she shook off Mrs. Napier's grip and rushed over. "I wondered if you might be ready to escort Mama and I home now?"

He blinked and wondered if Miss Hawthorne had sampled the ale today. He was not their escort. He'd come alone and intended to leave alone, too. "Where is your father?"

Miss Hawthorne bent close to whisper in his ear. "I need your help. Please don't argue."

He sighed. Most likely helping Miss Hawthorne involved describing some poor handsome fellow the girl must know everything about immediately. That was better done when no one could overhear her bold questions.

He considered the request. He'd spoken to Mrs. Grieves, offered his sympathy and support—not that she was alone in the world. There was little more he could do here today. "Very well."

He turned to Mrs. Beck, who had risen and was now looking at him through narrowed eyes. There were many who looked at him in that manner lately, often when Natalia Hawthorne was around, too.

He bowed to Mrs. Beck. "I am afraid you must excuse me. It seems I am needed elsewhere."

"I'm sure you are," Mrs. Beck murmured, a tight smile gracing her lips. "I look forward to seeing you again, sir."

"I am sure we will meet again soon," he agreed. He nodded to Mrs. Napier. "Good day, madam."

Miss Hawthorne wrapped her arm around his. "Goodbye, Mrs. Beck. Mrs. Napier."

"Miss Hawthorne," Mrs. Beck said with a tight nod.

Gideon allowed himself to be directed to the road before he spoke again. "That was hardly courteous. What's all this rush about?"

"You know exactly what I am about. I made a promise to myself to protect Lady Jessica's interests."

Jessica had been gone for months, and his life was a great deal quieter for her absence. "What promise?"

"The one that keeps you a bachelor."

He stopped the girl immediately. "The only promises exchanged were to help you find a worthy husband."

"Well, I made an amendment to the original

agreement without telling either of you. It's for the best, indeed. I mean to protect you from any lady who would try to take advantage of your kind nature." She frowned as her mother joined them. Mrs. Hawthorne was puffing, and Natalia Hawthorne released him at last to go to her side. "Are you all right, Mama?"

"Yes, indeed," she said, but she cast a sour expression toward the gathering of men drinking themselves into oblivion in the distance. Gideon noted Mr. Hawthorne quickly ducked out of sight.

"Mr. Whitfield has offered to escort us home, Mama. Isn't that wonderful news?"

Gideon tried not to roll his eyes at that lie. "I was on my way home already."

Mrs. Hawthorne, face more red than could be healthy, did not think to query her daughter's bold statement. "Oh, that is good news, because my dears, I am dead on my feet from this heat."

It wasn't that hot outside, and he exchanged a worried glance with Miss Hawthorne. Thankfully, the walk to the Hawthorne residence was a short one, and Mrs. Hawthorne disappeared inside almost as soon as he urged her to go.

Miss Hawthorne, however, lingered by the gate, eyes full of worry.

"Is your mother unwell?"

"Oh, Mama is fine. These spells come and go. Nothing to worry about, and I must thank you again for escorting us home today."

"And yet you are still frowning."

"I'm a little troubled." She looked at him a long moment, her expression assessing, before she spoke. "I realized today that you are a gentleman of such retiring habits that you may have become muddied about your appeal to the fairer sex."

Usually, Miss Hawthorne's sole concern when speaking to him was the appeal of other men, and how she might win them over. He stepped back from her quickly. "I do hope you have not now set your sights on me for a husband."

"I would never dare!" But then she sighed. "But I must warn you that *poor Mrs. Beck* is no grieving widow. She's said to be a *Merry Widow*. You know what that means, don't you? I overheard Mama and her friend Mrs. Clay talking about her yesterday. I think Mrs. Beck came to the wake with the express purpose of meeting you—our most eligible bachelor. Did you not think it odd that she was introduced to you first, sir, and did not approach Mrs. Grieves?"

He shook his head, astonished by such ridiculous speculation. "Mrs. Beck felt the heat today, too, and perhaps became distracted by my suggestion that she get some air. I'm certain she did not mean to give offense to Mrs. Grieves."

"She means to have you, I think." Miss Hawthorne raised one haughty brow. "I trust I do not need to spell that out for you, too."

"No, you do not," he said quite indignantly. "Where do you get these ridiculous notions?"

"Oh, do settle your feathers, Mr. Whitfield, and don't look at me as if I'm making this up. I know what I know and see. Mrs. Beck is a woman bent on seducing you."

He pinched the bridge of his nose, finding little to amuse him in the conversation. Natalia Hawthorne was turning into a managing sort of female. Just like her mother. "My private life is really none of your concern," he said firmly, hoping to end the discussion.

Miss Hawthorne straightened, eyes wide. "You are my friend's very good friend. You should be ashamed of yourself."

"Of what? I have done nothing." There was no reason Gideon had to live a chaste life, but he had chosen the path of bachelorhood years ago without regret. Natalia Hawthorne had no right to question his intentions if *he* did not. "And if I ever did *something* as you suggest I'm considering, it will be my own business entirely."

Miss Hawthorne frowned severely. "Lady

Jessica will not like this situation when she learns of it. It's her birthday."

Lady Jessica Westfall would be married to a peer by now, or very soon would be, and he would be content to know she'd be celebrating in fine company. "What happens in my personal life could hardly be of interest to the duke's daughter."

Chapter Two

———— ✦ ————

April 16th, 1819
Stapleton Manor

"I can assure you, Lord James and I will never make a match," Jessica insisted as she finished unpacking her possessions onto her dressing table at Stapleton Manor and then glanced around. "He's set to marry Lady Hannah Alexander within a fortnight, I'm sure."

Jessica's companion, Natalia Hawthorne, collapsed on the settee. "But I was so certain he'd offer for you. He was so attentive when he visited the estate at Christmas."

"Lord James found someone else to pay his addresses to very quickly it seems. Lady Hannah Alexander is very popular within the *ton*, especially with bachelors known to want a beautiful wife. She never lacked for a dance partner and is often surrounded by half a dozen gentlemen whenever not. *Her* season was bound to end in a marriage. I hardly saw him." Jessica shrugged. "Men are truly puzzling creatures. Saying one thing but then behaving another."

"They often do that," Natalia agreed.

"I thought we might at least have become friends once." However, once within the arms of the *ton*, Lord James had all but ignored her existence. "I shouldn't grumble that Lord James singled her out when I never really wanted him around. I'm actually impressed he chose with his heart rather than his purse, because he's in rather desperate need of funds to repair the tattered estate he's to inherit soon and her dowry was quite small."

"But I was sure he'd choose you."

"So was my family, but it seemed we were all wrong in the end. He liked her more." Jessica was glad for Lord James. The last thing she wanted to do was marry a fortune hunter. The last three month's in Town had wiped away her amusement with the polite world. She had seen and heard much in London that troubled her but she was, she supposed, at last seeing the world as it really was and not the fantasy everyone had told her to expect.

Natalia picked up a silk pillow and plumped it on her lap. "So you are back home for now, but how soon before you leave again?"

Jessica looked at her friend in surprise. "I've no intention of returning to London."

Natalia gaped. "But Jessica, your season has barely begun. You have to go back."

She sat close to Natalia on the settee. "I have done what my father wanted. I had the pleasure of seeing him and mother married in London, made my presentation, and danced and sampled the amusements of the great city. But as much as I wanted to please them, I was miserable the whole time I was away."

"Well, if I had my way, I'd never say no to a season in London, or a second or a third," Natalia promised with a rueful laugh.

"I know you wouldn't." She squeezed Natalia's hand. "And I've been thinking about this. If they force me to go back, I'll insist you and your mother join us in London. We'll find you a husband there."

Natalia hugged her. "Would you? Mother would be so excited. She's always talking about her one trip to London. I want to see the city, too, even if I never find a husband. I'd be forever in your debt for those memories."

"Now it's your turn. I want all the latest news of the district. Letters are much too brief to share all that must have happened since the week after Christmas."

Jessica, her father, and her future mother,

Gillian Thorpe, had left in something of a hurry in the first week of January, with tight lips about the real reason they were going to London so suddenly. Father's marriage had come as something of a surprise to many, but Jessica was proud to call Gillian mother. Her own had died when Jessica was very little, and she'd always felt the lack.

Natalia sat sideways on the settee to face Jessica. "Well, let me see. I told you about old Mr. Grieves passing. His wake lasted until well into the next day. There were…" Natalia leaned close to whisper some details that made Jessica's eyes widen in shock. "I couldn't put any of that in a letter. Father was so disguised after the wake that mother didn't speak to him for a whole week."

Jessica winced. "I'm sorry to hear your parents found another reason to quarrel."

"I'm growing used to it." Natalia shrugged. "Mr. Whitfield saw us home that day."

Jessica sat forward, eager for news of her neighbor. She hadn't spoken to Gideon Whitfield since January. That was unusual and not at all pleasant. "That was good of him."

"Mother was terribly fatigued."

"I trust Mrs. Hawthorne is in good health now," Jessica asked quickly. Natalia's mother was a sweet, motherly kind of woman, but had spent a considerable amount of time on her fainting couch before Christmas.

"Oh, yes. Mother promised it was just the heat of the day affecting her." Natalia scowled suddenly. "Mr. Whitfield has been very attentive while you were gone. He certainly kept his promise to you."

Jessica grinned. She'd asked Mr. Whitfield to keep an eye on Natalia while she'd been gone, make sure she stayed out of trouble and discreetly warn away any unsavory types. Natalia was much too fond of flirting with handsome scoundrels. "I'm glad."

"I wasn't," Natalia grumbled. "He proved too good at the task you set him, but we have not seen very much of him of lately though."

"He's not unwell, is he?" Jessica frowned. "Oh dear, and he has only Mrs. Mills and Mrs. Harrow to tend him. Mr. Lewis is next to useless as a valet. I'll ask Mother to call at Quigley Hill to see if there is anything we can do for him."

Natalia grabbed her hand and held her in place when she would have stood up and rushed off to find her new mother. "He's not ill."

Jessica subsided onto the settee with relief. "Well, why didn't you say so straight away? You know we worry about him. Mr. Whitfield is simply dreadful at taking care of himself, living alone the way he does, hardly enough servants to run the house efficiently."

A gentle smile played over Natalia's lips. "I am sorry I worried you. I thought perhaps you would have heard already, and that is why you returned early."

"Heard what? We only just arrived at home."

Natalia eased closer. "I thought you and Mr. Whitfield might have corresponded."

"No, of course we've not exchanged letters. That wouldn't be proper," Jessica protested. But she would have written him if she'd been allowed. "Father would have shared any news with me if it were important."

"Perhaps not about this matter." Natalia caught her hand and squeezed tightly. "Mr. Whitfield is expected to marry soon, my dear."

Jessica could only stare, blinded by shock and utter disbelief. "Nonsense. He's said he'd never marry a dozen times. Who is spreading such terrible gossip about him?"

"Well, everyone." Natalia sat back. "And it's not false speculation, either. Mrs. Napier's widowed sister has come to live with them, and I've seen her with Mr. Whitfield nearly every day since."

Whitfield married? Never in a million years would Jessica ever have imagined that. He was much too particular about…well, everything, especially his independence and privacy. Jessica narrowed her eyes. "Who is she?"

"Mrs. Alice Beck. She's a widow and has two sons to raise, so her sister brought her here to live with them. The boys are often running along the road to visit Quigley Hill."

Jessica shook her head again, dismissing the gossip as idle speculation. "Mr. Whitfield is very tolerant of children."

"He has dined with Mrs. Beck."

Jessica stilled. "He hosted a dinner at Quigley Hill?"

"No, nothing so obvious as that." Natalia peered at her. "Not yet, anyway."

"Good. The last time Mr. Whitfield tried to host a dinner, Mr. Lewis lit too many candles in the dining room. That carelessness spoiled a beautiful table cloth and could have burned down the house." Jessica jumped to her feet and rooted around in her small trunk until she found the present she'd purchased for Natalia. She turned, smiling, and held out the package. "Now before I forget again, Happy Birthday, for last month."

Natalia shrieked. "You remembered!"

"Of course I remembered." Jessica hugged Natalia quickly. "You're one of my best friends."

"My turn." Natalia lifted her shawl from the settee, revealing a small parcel lying beneath. "Happy Birthday for *this* month."

Jessica laughed and untied her present in a

rush. Natalia had gifted her a piece of embroidery. Her needlework was as always very fine, much better than Jessica's varied attempts. "This is perfect."

Natalia rushed to untie her package then. Inside, she would discover a pair of elegant evening gloves and a matching silk shawl. Each item was purchased, but Jessica hoped she would love them just the same.

Natalia held each up to the light from the window to view them better. "Oh, my!"

"Do you like them? I know they're a little plain, but I'm sure you can embroider something on each if you like."

"I wouldn't change a thing about them." Natalia wiped at her eyes quickly. "This is too much."

"Nonsense." But Jessica's eyes misted with tears, too. "Every lady should have a perfect pair of evening gloves and a pretty shawl to wrap around her shoulders. Especially one trying to attract a husband."

Natalia laughed dismissively. "My prospects are still quite slim, but I'm sure the addition of these gloves and a silk shawl will increase my appeal tremendously. Thank you."

"You're very welcome." They hugged again, and everything was almost right with Jessica's world. She was home but she had one more birthday gift to deliver—to Mr. Whitfield—

before the end of the day.

Unfortunately, Giddy simply hated anyone to make a fuss about his birthday. He tended to become embarrassed when the subject of his growing older was mentioned, too. More so if an event was made of his birthday with any sort of celebration.

Mr. Whitfield had arrived in the world on the twenty-ninth day of February, a date that occurred once every four years. He was only seven years old, if one only counted those occasions. Once he'd said he'd gone eight whole years between birthday celebrations. That sounded ghastly to Jessica, who found any excuse to celebrate important events.

Regardless of the lack of February twenty-nine this year, Jessica felt the month of his birth should be marked with a present, now that she was old enough to have pin money of her own to spend.

Natalia tugged on her gown to reclaim her attention. "You seem no different after your season. I thought you might have changed."

"I may have traveled, but I am still the same woman I was before," Jessica promised. But she was a young woman armed with a great deal more knowledge of men than when she'd left her home. The few days she'd spent with her older sister Fanny while Mother and Father celebrated their marriage alone had opened her eyes to another world of secrets and seductions. Fanny, an independent widow, and her friends had talked openly about gentlemen they liked, spoke of making love in a way that suggested all of them enjoyed their lovers immensely. Fanny, too, enjoyed a more liberal existence than Jessica had ever known was possible for a woman.

"Good. I had hoped we'd still be as close as we were becoming at Christmas. It's been so dull around here without you." Natalia leaned forward. "Now, I have been waiting with great patience, but please, tell me everything about London. What was it like?"

"Dirty and noisy," she answered without hesitation.

"I meant the gentlemen vying for your hand, silly," Natalia chided.

Jessica wrinkled her nose. "I knew what you meant, and my answer is still the same."

Natalia chortled with laughter. "So the gentlemen in London are no different to their country cousins."

Jessica winced. "There was very little difference and few who deserve the term gentleman."

Natalia arched her brow. "Was there no one like Mr. Whitfield to charm you with talk of fungus at dinner?"

Gideon Whitfield it seemed was unique

among men. Clever. Witty. Dependable. "None at all. Many titled lords speak only of horses, wagers and politics. They smother themselves in perfumes and reek of cigar by night's end."

Natalia's expression grew serious once more. "You never said if you'd found a man to marry there."

"I did not," she admitted.

"Out of all of London's most eligible bachelors?"

She rubbed her brow. "Please do not be cross with me, too."

"Oh, I'm not. Never that. But I am disappointed that none could see the jewel you are. Are your parents very upset with you? Or is it your sister stirring the pot again?"

She shrugged, feeling foolish and awkward. "Mother and Father have never said they were disappointed in me, but the way their smiles diminished each morning when we talked of any potential suitors is hint enough that they were concerned by my lack of success."

"Then why have you come home so early? I wasn't expecting you to return for another month at least. Were you involved in a scandal? Did you kiss someone you should not have?"

"No." Jessica laughed softly and answered only Natalia's first question. "My father brought us home to surprise Gillian with the arrival of her brother and family tomorrow, but he is so terrible at keeping secrets that I knew well before we left London what we were coming home for."

Natalia's smile diminished. "So you'll be too busy with guests to see much of anyone."

"Not too busy to see you," she promised. "Mr. and Mrs. Garland have two sons, both younger than eight years old. I will not be required to amuse them. I expect Gillian will want to spend every spare moment getting to know her family again. She has not seen them for a very long time."

Natalia smiled broadly. "The duke is so sweet to arrange that. Mama has been positively gloating—knowing about the marriage before everyone else read the announcement posted in the village. I never thought his grace would wed again, least of all your beloved companion."

"I'm delighted he did, because my father in love is very amusing."

"I am glad. For years everyone had talked about how Stapleton needed a duchess again. Well," Natalia began as she regained her feet. "If you have visitors coming, I'd better make myself scarce. Send me a note when I can come to visit you again, and then when the fuss has died down and you're free, we can talk properly about all the handsome young men you kissed while you were away."

Jessica's cheeks grew warm.

Natalia hugged her again and fortunately never saw Jessica's discomfort. "I have missed you, Jess. I want to hear every delicious detail about your suitors when I see you next. Thank you again for the gifts."

"It's my pleasure," Jessica promised. "Thank you for mine. I know just what to use the embroidery for."

Natalia rushed out, and Jessica sank onto the settee beneath her window again, her thoughts on her uncertain future.

There had been no one she had wanted to encourage in London. There was not one single gentleman who had tried to steal a kiss from her, either. She was starting to worry there was something wrong with her. Half the young women she'd met in London were either married or engaged or being seriously courted. The others, women with pitifully small dowries, had better experiences to share with their friends about their season than Jessica would ever have. Her season had been a resounding failure all round.

Chapter Three

———◆———

Gideon ran up the long flight of steps to Stapleton Manor on Saturday afternoon and knocked on the heavy oak door. He'd only just learned the duke's family had returned the day before. It wasn't normal for him to be so late calling on his friend. But he'd indulged in a great deal too much port at dinner last night with the Napiers and, as a consequence of it, he'd slept until midday.

The butler admitted him, all smiles. "Good afternoon, Mr. Whitfield. His grace expected to see you yesterday."

"Mr. Brown." He rushed to remove his hat and gloves then handed them over. "I'm sure he did."

"The family is in the drawing room with their guests."

Gideon hesitated in the act of smoothing

his wavy hair. "Guests?"

Mr. Brown nodded. "The duke arranged for the surprise visit of her grace's brother, wife, and children."

He smiled but took a step back. "Perhaps I should return another time."

A soft step sounded behind him. "Why would you believe you were not wanted today, Mr. Whitfield?"

Gideon pivoted slowly at the sound of Lady Jessica's voice, his heart skipping a beat as he spotted her slender form moving toward him.

"I'll see Mr. Whitfield to my father, Mr. Brown," she murmured.

Jessica glided soundlessly across the parquetry, lips lifting at the corners—as if she had a secret she wanted to tell him. He'd seen that look so many times that his anticipation grew the nearer she came.

"Jess." He said her name softly, because he should not use the diminutive form where a servant might hear. She did not seem very changed at first glance. Her uncovered dark hair was intricately coiled upon her head, her body elegantly swathed in yards of muslin.

A huge smile burst over her face as she stopped before him. Her hazel eyes glowed with happiness, and he bowed as Jess dipped into a perfect curtsy. He drank in her smiles and his heart lightened. Jessica had always been a happy child, and he was glad to see her months away had not changed that. She exuded confidence and good health, as ever.

His eyes dropped to a paper-wrapped package that crackled as she shifted it to her left hip. Jessica was always busy, always involved in some activity for the estate rather than idle mischief. No doubt he would find out about the contents of that package eventually.

"Father expected you to call yesterday, Giddy. So did I. Where have you been, sir!"

Her tone was slightly accusing, and he rushed to explain his absence. "I was late rising today and only just learned of your return. Forgive me, my lady."

He reached for her hand. There was the slightest hesitation before her bare fingers slipped delicately over his calloused ones. Gideon squeezed her hand and then let her go. "I don't wish to intrude on the reunion. I can come back another day."

"And miss all the fun? Never." Jess laughed. "Mama most definitely wants you to meet her brother while he is here. You will enjoy the stories Mr. Garland has shared about their childhood already this morning. I've been laughing so hard my sides hurt."

He smiled at the mention of the new Duchess of Stapleton, a woman who had been Lady Jessica's companion the last time they'd all been together. "Mama, is it?"

Jessica nodded decisively. "She's the only mother I'll ever know."

He smiled despite the loss Jess had suffered as a child. She had never known her own mother, but had been raised by her grieving father, quarreling sisters and a string of efficient nurses. "Then we did a good thing last winter."

Her eyes lit up with pleasure at the reminder of their combined matchmaking efforts for her father and beloved companion. It was an inspired idea, to help the duke admit his feelings had grown for Mrs. Gillian Thorpe beyond those of a mere employer, but it had required Jessica's assistance and not a little private planning to pull it off. "We did indeed. Father has been made very happy by his marriage."

Jessica's smile dimmed slightly, and she set her package aside on a side table. She rested her hand on it a moment but then shook her head. "Come, Mr. Whitfield. His grace is eager to see you."

Clearly whatever was contained in the parcel was unimportant. Gideon was almost disappointed, but when Jessica hooked her arm through his, Gideon couldn't remain so as he looked down on her.

Jessica was not particularly tall, the top of her head barely reaching his shoulder. Gideon had watched over this girl—woman, he corrected himself—since she'd been a child, escorting her about when her father and siblings had been occupied elsewhere. She was out in society now. Eighteen at last and obviously quite assured.

He dragged his attention away from her as they stepped into the drawing room together.

The Duke of Stapleton sprang to his feet immediately, a smile as welcoming as Jessica's beaming across the room. "About time, sir."

"Your grace, welcome home," he said, releasing Jessica so he could bow.

"None of that nonsense," Stapleton exclaimed, rushing up to shake his hand vigorously. "Make yourself at home as you usually do."

"As you wish," he said as he hid his relief. He'd never assume he'd always be welcome, but he liked Stapleton very much, even if Gideon was a good deal younger than the duke, though with none of the status of a title to add to his distinction. Gideon studied his neighbor closely, noting his ease and appearance of good health. Stapleton must be pleased by the changes in his life by the look of it, too. He pounded Gideon's shoulder suddenly with the excitement of a much younger man, and that made him laugh. "It's good to see you again."

"Likewise," the duke replied then gestured beside him.

Gideon turned to the new Duchess of Stapleton, formerly known as Mrs. Gillian Thorpe. "Your grace," he said as he bowed deeply to the woman the duke had fallen head over heels in love with.

"Dear Whitfield," she exclaimed, as she moved forward to take his hands. The duchess kissed both his cheeks in welcome. "Our truest friend."

He grinned, though a little embarrassed by her warm welcome. The woman was positively glowing at him, but she looked paler than she'd formerly been. "I must say, marriage suits you."

Her eyes sparkled briefly. "So says the man who made my happiness possible."

He inclined his head. "It was not all my doing."

He looked toward Jessica, but she'd already moved away. She sat primly on a single chair, watching him from a distance with a happy smile. He returned it, and then turned back to the duchess. "I had a willing accomplice."

"Oh, I know only too well the collusion you pair must have managed behind my back. And, no matter who dares to claim credit, I am very grateful," her grace promised. She gestured to the couple standing behind her. "May I introduce my younger brother, Lincoln Garland, and his wife, Mrs. Hazel Garland? Their children are currently taking refreshments in the nursery."

"They will empty the duchess' vast kitchen if we are not careful, and run her poor servants ragged I fear," Garland added, and then laughed good-naturedly as they shook hands. The fellow was tall, lanky even, and Gideon could see a strong resemblance to the duchess when Garland smiled.

"Welcome, Mr. Garland. Mrs. Garland. How long are you staying with their graces?"

"A few days at best," Mrs. Garland murmured in a soft tone that revealed a woman of intelligence and polite manners. "My husband must return to his employment soon, but we could not miss this chance to meet my husband's sister and discover how well she has done for herself. You have our gratitude, too, for bringing her back into our lives through her marriage to such a kind and gracious man."

"Ah, I see Stapleton has you well fooled already," Gideon teased, then grinned cheekily at Stapleton when he spluttered. "Wait till Christmas comes around, and you will see his grace's true colors."

"They see me as I really am, while you notice only fabrications of your vivid imagination," the duke exclaimed. "And besides, I have changed my mind about the necessity of winter festivities. Great good can come from hanging mistletoe about the place."

Stapleton caught his wife's hand and kissed the back of it passionately.

Jessica laughed. "He says that now, but in December, he was raging the halls and complaining about the stuff!"

The duchess clucked her tongue. "Can you blame him? You two are nothing but trouble when you are together," she chided.

Gideon pasted an innocent smile on his face because it was all too true that he and Jessica had been the ones hanging it up behind the duke's back. They'd had great fun doing it, too. And then Jessica managed to slip some into her father's pocket one evening, and a romance with Gillian had bloomed without help from then on.

Mr. Garland chuckled. "Mr. Whitfield, I am in your debt then, too. We have much to talk about, I think."

Her grace laughed. "Please do not give my brother any ideas for when he visits us at Christmas. He used to play the most horrid tricks on me when we were young."

Gideon liked the Garlands very much. They seemed like good people. "How convenient to have met a solicitor who might feel indebted to me."

Garland raised one brow. "My gratitude only goes so far, sir."

Gideon laughed and moved to sit on the

empty chair nearest Jessica. "Definitely a relation of yours, your grace. Just as mistrustful as you have always been of me."

Garland laughed and slapped his thigh. "I easily see now why you are so loved at Stapleton Manor, Mr. Whitfield. You amuse with hardly any effort."

"The ladies must love his company," Mrs. Garland teased, throwing a shy smile in his direction. "But is it true no one yet has claimed your heart?"

He straightened his waistcoat to hide his discomfort that the conversation had turned to his bachelor status already. "Obviously."

Mrs. Garland shook her head. "Such a shame."

"I'm much too old and set in my ways for marriage now." He hoped the subject would end there.

The duke barked out a laugh. "At least until his head is finally turned. Then like every other unwed fellow, he will plunge into a pursuit with blinkers on and not think of the consequences for his life until it is too late," the duke warned. "If only he'd fallen for one of my daughters, he would have been my favorite son-in-law," the duke complained. "As it is, I must wait until he yearns for company and visits."

Gideon tried not to wince. There had once been an unspoken expectation that Gideon might make a match with one of the duke's older daughters. Thankfully, they had married men better suited to their temperaments. "I came as soon as I learned you were home."

The duke looked on him fondly. "I suppose I must believe you, but no doubt you've never lacked company in our absence."

As he was about to refute that claim, Jessica suddenly sprang to her feet.

"If you will excuse me," she murmured. "I have something I must attend to."

He was disappointed she would go so soon, but it was not unexpected. Jessica was an energetic sort, always running off somewhere.

They settled in to chat, and he listened to the duchess and her brother attempt to catch up on years of news in the space of an hour. The duke and duchess shared tidbits about their adventures in London, too, but he couldn't help but notice there was no mention of a wedding for Jessica, or even a courtship underway. They said nothing of Jessica's future, but perhaps they would not speak of it openly yet.

The duchess caught his eye. "Will you join us for dinner, Mr. Whitfield?"

Gideon glanced at the duke when the question registered fully. He had to decline. "If I'd known you were coming home so early, I would not have arranged for my own dinner party to be held tonight. It is much too late to alter the invitations or postpone the gathering."

"We would not want you to alter anything on our account," the duchess assured him, "but I am sure Lady Jessica will be disappointed not to have your company at dinner."

"I'm sure she will not miss me very much," he promised as he checked the time. "And I am afraid I really must take my leave now."

Though they begged him to stay a little longer, Gideon had no choice but to say goodbye. He was determined that all was in readiness for his first dinner party in years and that nothing was left to chance.

He exited the manor via the front door but, having come on foot, he took the most direct path home—a path that ran alongside Jessica's little greenhouse. He would say a private farewell if she were there. If not, he would hear about her season tomorrow.

He found her, talking to her plants once again. She dearly loved the greenhouse her father had gifted her with and, if left to her own agenda, would spend the bulk of the day coaxing them to grow with soft words of encouragement. "I hoped I would find you here."

"Yes," she said with a sad smile. "I am nothing if not predictable."

He moved to stand near her, worried by her

changed demeanor from her earlier happiness. He'd never known her to be sad at seeing him before. "Something is wrong. What is it?"

"Nothing." She let out a shaky breath, turned away and, when she turned back, she had that parcel in her hands again. "Happy birthday."

He shook his head. "It is not my birthday this year."

She thrust the parcel at him anyway. "I don't care what the calendar says. Everyone deserves a birthday present each year."

He smiled at her stubborn insistence that he celebrate his growing older. Her confusion over his birthdate was one of his fondest memories. Being born on the twenty-ninth day of February, a day that only arrived every four years, perplexed a great many of his acquaintances at first.

"I don't have a present for you," he confessed quietly.

He'd considered it, but dismissed the notion almost immediately. Now he felt he should have gotten her something, even if it were only a new plant for her collection.

"Just seeing you again is present enough," Jess promised, shaking him by the arm. "I wanted to spend my pin money on someone dear to me."

He slowly turned the parcel over in his

hands, noticing it contained something soft inside. Since presents were rare in his life, he liked to try to guess and draw out the moment for as long as possible. Today, he was baffled.

"Well, open it," she insisted.

He set the parcel down on a worktable and pulled on the little string bow. Working slowly, he pulled the paper aside. He blinked...and then shook out a large dark blue garment. "Jessica! Is this a gentleman's banyan?"

"It is. Do you like the material?"

It was a very personal item to receive from anyone, and costly, too. He rubbed the dark blue brocade between his finger and thumb, then held the garment away from him to judge if it would fit him. It seemed large enough. "You should never have spent your pin money on me."

"Try it on for me."

He glanced around, but they were of course alone inside the greenhouse.

He swallowed, realizing that coming here was unwise. He should not be alone with her anymore. Anyone who found them alone together might get the wrong idea. Jess was no longer a little girl. "I cannot."

She laughed softly. "Well, I can't very well follow you home to see it on you there."

"No, you most definitely should not do that," Gideon exclaimed. "I have guests expected for dinner tonight."

Jess stared at him with a concerned expression rather than the excitement he'd expected. "You will keep Mr. Lewis away from the candles this time, won't you?"

He grinned and tweaked her nose. "Don't worry, I'll be lighting them myself."

He glanced behind him, and then decided there would be no real harm if he tried on the garment so Jessica could see him in it just this once, if he were quick. He stripped off his brown coat and slipped his arms into the full sleeves of the blue banyan. Jessica assisted, standing behind him and smoothing the fabric over his shoulders.

Once the garment was in place, he turned to face her to get her opinion. "Well? How do I look?"

She sighed a little wistfully. "Exactly as I imagined. Blue has always suited you."

Feeling a little warm from the compliment, he dropped his gaze and tried to see himself. He smoothed his hands down the beautiful material. The sleeves ended in deep, wide cuffs, and there were two pockets—one to carry his new eyeglasses in and the other a spare. He did not do up the buttons but they began at his neck and stopped midway down his thighs. The overall length was perfect, ending halfway along his calves. The inside was lined with patterned silk, and it was obviously quite expensive.

It was an astonishing gift, and he couldn't hold back his happiness at receiving something so unique. "Thank you, Jess. This is the most beautiful gift I've ever received."

"It is my pleasure," she said, brushing her fingers against the sleeve of the garment. Her fingers moved up and covered his forearm. She squeezed him tightly. "This one will be perfect to wear for the coming winter, too."

He covered her hand where it sat on his sleeve. "And people always say old bachelors must fend for themselves. I am astonished you remembered my birthday with all the excitement your season must have been. Did your father help you purchase this?"

"No. My brother was in London for a week, and he accompanied me shopping."

"Which brother?"

"Samuel, of course." She drew back. "We pretended it was a gift for him so the shopkeeper could not outright refuse to serve me. You're about the same size."

"I'll have to thank him next time I see him, but I have to say, I always worry when you and your brother get together."

She laughed softly. "Samuel was on his best behavior, I swear, so you have no cause to worry." She sighed—an exhalation he loved to hear. "It was no trouble to buy you a birthday present for once."

"Once, but never again," he warned. It wasn't at all proper that she had singled him out. He bent close, intending to place a brotherly kiss on her forehead, as he'd done when Christmas gifts had been exchanged in past years. "Thank you, Jess."

As he dropped his head, and Jessica's chin lifted high until she was looking directly into his eyes. He froze, inches away from kissing her on the lips by mistake—something he'd never done and never should. His heart started to pound very hard against his ribs as time stood still.

Jessica might be out but she was destined for another. No doubt she'd had dozens of suitors all vying for her hand in marriage—and kisses.

Her eyes widened slowly. There was no way to pretend he hadn't been about to kiss her, so he cupped her face and tilted her head down to place a chaste one on her forehead as originally intended.

"I should take my leave," he murmured.

"Enjoy your dinner." Jessica nodded, but a frown now added a deep groove between her brows.

He resisted the urge to brush the mark away with thumb. "I hope it goes well. Good evening."

"Until tomorrow, Giddy."

Gideon hurried out of the greenhouse.

He was nearly home when he realized his mistake. He stopped, looked down at his clothing and cursed. He had rushed from the Stapleton estate wearing the banyan Jessica had given him for his birthday.

He spun about and slapped a hand to his forehead. He'd left his coat behind, too, along with his hat and gloves and new glasses. He didn't have time to run back to Jessica's greenhouse now. He'd have to return for them after the dinner or make do without them until tomorrow morning. What an absentminded old fool he must seem!

Chapter Four

———◆———

Stapleton Manor was home, and yet Jessica felt decidedly out of sorts as she emerged from her bedchamber early the following morning after a restless sleep. She walked the silent halls briskly, increasing the distance between her and the bedchambers of her parents and also of their guests, so she did not disturb anyone.

They had all stayed up very late last night becoming acquainted with the Garlands. Mama had alternated between laughter and tears all night. Mr. Garland had struggled for many years, and it was only because he had met Mrs. Garland that his situation had changed for the better. The couple were very happily matched, and their children polite and charming.

Nevertheless, she rushed down the main staircase and breathed a sigh of relief to be alone. It was not that she disliked the idea of seeing people in the morning; she loved her parents very dearly. But they were newly married, in the habit of kissing and embracing quite often, which could be somewhat awkward to be around.

She longed to know what it felt like to kiss a man, not that she could tell anyone that.

And she had almost been kissed yesterday, she was sure.

The frustration of missing out was painfully embarrassing.

She crossed the hall, singing out a good morning to any servant she passed. They were used to her ways, pleasant to talk to, but they were not her friends. She could not confide in them the way she could her family or closest friends, and that meant she was often at a loose end. In London particularly, she'd had little to do during the day when not attending parties. Hardly anyone to talk to about her hopes and dreams.

She burst out onto the rear terrace and stopped to drink in the view of the manicured gardens. Her first task was to take a brisk walk around the manor, and then to bring her greenhouse plants to order again before they departed for Sunday services in the nearby village chapel at ten o'clock.

She strolled along familiar paths and neatly clipped lawn, smiling at everything and everyone she passed. The gardeners had looked after everything beautifully in their absence, of course, but they did not love her own plants the way she did. They simply refused to talk to them.

The greenhouse was the only corner of Stapleton that was considered her responsibility.

On an impulse, she made a slight detour. She followed the path toward the brook that separated Stapleton estate and Quigley Hill, Gideon's property, and looked with longing at the stone footbridge that would allow her to cross over. Gideon's gardens had always fascinated her.

There was always something new to see flowering along the brook's edge during the warmer months, and she lingered there, starved for familiar sights. Quigley's gardens were wild and magnificent in spring, and during winter, the walled garden archways dripped icicles that caught the light. She had spent two whole hours roaming those chilly paths on her own at age six and been roundly scolded for the trouble she'd caused everyone who'd been searching for her.

When Giddy had found her standing on his front steps, shivering, she'd been taken inside to warm herself before the drawing-room fire while Father was informed to call off the search. That had been her first trip into Quigley Hill, but not her last. Father did not know how often she'd crossed that boundary following butterflies or birds, and Gideon thankfully never tattled on her.

She crossed the bridge and entered Quigley land. She smiled as she brushed her finger over Gideon's lavender hedges, planted along the garden paths many years ago, well before the time she knew what lavender even was. He and his father before him had planted so many fragrant plants, and she'd long used the bounty of Quigley gardens for making scented sachets for herself.

She picked some as she went, knowing she had permission if it was not wasted, and looked ahead as the roofline of Giddy's house came into view. She stopped in the shade of an Elm tree to admire its familiar pleasing shape.

The house was a great deal smaller than Stapleton Manor. Only four bedchambers upstairs, with Gideon as the sole occupant, and five public rooms below—a drawing room, dining room, morning room, Gideon's study, and another unused room. The servants toiled on the distant east side of the ground floor and slept in the attic space above.

Jessica loved the place for its simplicity and grace. She was always finding something new to look at and smile about. Giddy's ancestors were more conservative and modest than her own. The gardens, too, reflected their owners' tastes—a series of walled enclosures, intersected with straight paths but filled to the brim with plants of every description by Gideon and his gardeners.

She crossed two enclosures before she could spy the lower windows of the house.

The French doors to Gideon's drawing room were open to allow the breeze to enter. Believing him to be home, she decided to speak to him before continuing on her walk.

A flash of blue across the grounds caught her eye and, expecting Giddy, she turned, lifting her hand to wave. She froze instead.

A woman wearing blue, a stranger with dark hair and pale skin, was strolling beneath the trees at Gideon's side.

Jessica darted inside the nearest walled garden before she was seen where she ought not to be without a chaperone.

Hearing no footsteps or anyone calling out to her, she risked a peek around the open archway. She was in luck; Gideon and his visitor appeared not to have noticed her at all. They were still some distance away and not looking in her direction. Unfortunately, there was only one way out of this particular walled garden, and while Gideon would not scold her, Jessica had no choice but to remain where she was until the stranger went away.

Jessica inhaled her scented flowers as Gideon and the woman continued to talk. What they said, she couldn't hear, but Gideon laughed suddenly.

He held out his hand, and the lady shook it.

And then the woman laid her hands on Gideon's waistcoat and stretched up on her toes to kiss him full on the lips.

Jessica covered her mouth with both hands to hold in the gasp of shock that would reveal her presence to Gideon and the woman.

She had not believed Natalia's tale held any truth yesterday. But here it was. Right before her.

Gideon Whitfield *was* courting someone at last!

———◆———

"What was that for?" Gideon asked as Mrs. Beck drew back from kissing him without warning.

"I…I thought…" she began, but then frowned, as if unsure how to account for her actions. "We've been spending so much time together."

"Indeed. You asked to see the gardens, and I am always happy to show anyone about."

"Yes, indeed. They are quite lovely. Everything you promised and more."

He drew back from her. "I'm glad you like them. I'm very proud of what I've achieved so far this year."

"Yes, well. I do enjoy coming here with the children," Mrs. Beck promised, although she seemed uncomfortable now. "You have every right to be proud."

He cleared his throat. "I wonder where your sons have gone? It seems ominously quiet."

"I should go and look for them," she suggested. "Unless…"

Unless he was interested in kissing her again? He wasn't in the least. Better not to raise her expectations. Kissing Mrs. Beck, or having her kiss him, hadn't been unpleasant, but he hoped she would not attempt to do so again. He was a gentleman, and not one for casual dalliances or leading ladies on. "I had better come along, in case the youngest has climbed a tree again and needs help returning to the ground."

She settled her hand on her belly and nodded. A blush seemed to be climbing her cheeks, too. Had she imagined an enthusiastic response to her bold behavior? He wouldn't marry her, so he shouldn't kiss her. He wasn't a scoundrel.

"I do hope he's not stuck again," Mrs. Beck

murmured. "You were so good to help him down the last time."

"It was no bother to help. Boys are always getting into one scrape after another." He gestured to the narrow path. "After you, madam."

When the path widened again, far beyond the limits of his well-tended garden where they could walk side-by-side, he surveyed the green paddock of long grass before them carefully and put his hands behind his back. "No sign yet."

"They would not have gone home without me," she said in a worried tone.

"No, I imagine they would not. Perhaps they are playing hide and seek."

Mrs. Beck drew close until her arm brushed his. "I wanted to thank you again for the pleasurable dinner last night. I almost forgot I was a widow and living with my sister and husband for a while."

Last night's early success had soured later on. "I'm glad you enjoyed yourself. I did, too, but I am sorry that your brother-in-law's consumption of spirits made him coarse when he spoke with you."

She shrugged. "I will learn to ignore it in due time."

He sighed. "I promised myself not to meddle, and I know it is none of my business, but after last night, I must ask how long you intend to live with the Napiers?"

"Forever, I fear. My pocket is more than a little empty at present," she confessed with obvious embarrassment. "I have no other option."

"You could remarry," he murmured—and then he blinked. "Oh! Was that why you kissed me? To see…"

She tossed her head. "I can see now that I made a mistake."

"I apologize if I have made you think I felt more for you than I do."

She nodded, and then jutted out her chin. "No. The mistake was mine. Let us not speak of it again."

He sighed and scanned the empty field again for the boys with a heavy heart. He had "bumped" into Mrs. Beck every day in recent weeks. He wondered, not for the first time, if she had planted herself and her children in his path quite deliberately. Natalia Hawthorne had suggested she might but until today they had never been more than just polite to each other. They hardly knew each other. "Tell me how Napier speaks to you at home?"

She shook her head. "There is nothing you can do."

He shook his head, recalling Mrs. Napier's recent flattery. "Is he the one urging you to seduce me or is it your own sister?"

"He never suggested it." She shook her head. "Not directly, but it is plain as day that he doesn't want us there."

So not the brother-in-law but perhaps the sister was trying to push them together. Well, he wasn't having that. "And the boys? How are they being treated?"

"Not well." Her face contorted with grief but she managed not to shed a tear. "They are both very hard on them. Napier's always shouting at them for one reason or another."

"They shouldn't suffer."

"I know. There is no help for it. All I can do is keep them busy, away from him, and hope not for a repeat of last evening."

He looked at her sharply. "What else happened last night?"

Mrs. Beck looked away. "My sons were punished for offering disrespect to Mrs. Napier."

"I see," he said. "Did they deserve it?"

"For rushing past her to say good night to me? No, they certainly did not. The punishment far exceeded what was needed to teach them to walk more slowly in the house," she said through gritted teeth. "All they will learn from him is how to become a monster."

He looked down at Mrs. Beck, shocked by her confession. "How badly are they hurt?"

"Enough. My brother-in-law has taken a

dislike to my youngest son, since he looks most like my late husband."

"I'd like to see their injuries." Gideon's stomach clenched with anxiety, though. He'd known the Napiers were hard people, but the youngest boy was barely six years old. "Should I have owned a cottage in the village, I would have been happy to offer it to you to live in. Since I don't, I urge you to look further afield for new lodgings as soon as you can."

She cleared her throat. "You really don't think that you and I might suit?"

"No," he said firmly to discourage her. He hardly knew Mrs. Beck, and he was certainly not falling in love with her. He felt compassion for her situation, concern for her sons to be growing up without protection. But he could not replace their father. "I prefer my solitary existence, but I do not mind the occasional interruption, such as their visit today. They are safe here, I assure you."

She gulped and nodded. "I thought perhaps you might be lonely of living alone."

He relished his solitude. "No."

Mrs. Beck moved away to a section of post and rail fence. She leaned upon it, staring into the distance. "I could bear living on my sister's charity if not for the boys' unhappiness."

"Perhaps you could take up a useful profession? I understand you've had a good education. There has not been a tutor in the district for quite some time, and there are a great many girls in need of guidance. Letter writing, accounting for the home expenses and such."

Mrs. Beck's eyes lit up at the idea but then her smile faded. "I can hardly imagine my sister agreeing to let students into her home."

"Ah, I had not considered the matter that far. But you would need only a little space, somewhere quiet." He frowned as he considered the buildings closest to the village green, the most central point in the district. The tavern boasted a private dining room, but there would be considerable noise to distract any students and the expense of renting the space might be too great. Gideon had more free space at Quigley Hill, but his home was on the opposite side of the village and any potential students for Mrs. Beck. A place in the village would be preferable.

Surely there must be a place somewhere that could be rented.

And then he recalled Lady Jessica had inherited her old aunt's cottage in the village on her eighteenth birthday.

The cottage was currently empty, but never stayed that way for long. Gideon had no idea what plans Jessica might have for the dwelling. But he could inquire on Mrs. Beck's behalf.

The aunt who had owned it had once offered instruction to the village girls, too, for a time. Jessica might be interested in supporting such a venture; at least until she married and her husband's wishes took precedence over her own. "Would you leave the matter with me for a few days?"

"You have an idea that might help us get away from my sister and her husband?"

"Perhaps. But I can say no more for now. I will make some inquiries and let you know if there is hope."

She looked at him curiously but nodded, too. "Very well. I shall place my trust in you, sir."

A pair of blond heads suddenly sprung up from the long grass. "You didn't try to find us very hard!"

Mrs. Beck slipped through the post and rail fence and ran to her children. She kissed the tops of their heads, clearly a devoted mother. "I'm sorry, my darlings. Mr. Whitfield and I were talking."

The youngest clung to his mother's skirts but cradled his hand against his chest. Gideon took a step in his direction. The little fellow did not smile at Gideon. He never had.

"Hello, Thomas."

The boy looked up at his mother. "Are you going to marry him?"

"Gracious, no," Mrs. Beck chided quickly. "Mr. Whitfield would, however, like to look at your sore fingers."

The eldest pulled the youngest behind him and glared. "I won't let anyone hurt him again."

Gideon strolled forward, conscious that the boys looked at him with painful wariness. He did not blame them for their caution. "You are a good brother to want to protect Thomas. I would never harm him. But if you'd prefer, my housekeeper tends all my scratches and scrapes, and will be very gentle with your brother. You can go with him into the house of course."

Although both looked skeptical, they followed their mother when she called them to come with her. Gideon placed his hands behind his back and strolled slowly toward his home. He led them inside to the housekeeper's room and bade them wait there while he found his servants.

Mrs. Harrow and Mrs. Mills were seated at the kitchen table, sipping tea. "Do you have a moment to tend a few scratches?"

"Are you hurt, sir?"

"Not I. Mrs. Beck's youngest, and perhaps the other one, too. You might have to cajole them a little to find out more."

Mrs. Harrow and Mrs. Mills exchanged a long look. "As you like, sir."

"I've left them in your room, Mrs. Harrow,"

he murmured. The pair gathered their things, and a plate of biscuits, and rushed out. He heard the soft exclamations of his servants and paced the kitchen until they returned.

Mrs. Harrow drew close. "Mrs. Beck had to go but wished us to bid you goodbye, sir."

"Good."

Mrs. Harrow frowned. "Those wounds?"

Gideon rubbed his fingers over his palm, remembering his own hard childhood. Thankfully, he bore no lasting scars from his father's punishments. But he remembered them all, the unfairness and ferocity.

"A switch," Mrs. Harrow informed him sadly.

"Just like my father did to me."

Mrs. Harrow patted his arm. "That's all in the past, sir."

"If only I could forget as easily," he said quietly.

Mrs. Mills returned to her chair nearest the hearth, her expression understanding. "If you don't mind me saying, perhaps a visit to Stapleton Manor will chase the ghosts away. His grace usually cheers you up."

He nodded. "Yes, perhaps a visit with friends is just what I need."

Chapter Five

———•———

Jessica dragged in a deep breath. It did not help. The idea that Giddy had kissed that woman, a stranger, offended her sensibilities so much, she clenched her hands into fists. Had he not, just yesterday afternoon, declared he was too old for marriage?

Obviously he wasn't too old to kiss strangers. Jessica had never known him to pay any attention to other ladies, but then Mrs. Garland's teasing comments yesterday about his popularity flooded her mind, as did some of Natalia's previous remarks. Gideon Whitfield was good-looking, wealthy in a limited fashion, which no doubt made him a prize—more so than she'd ever considered. Did he behave differently when she was not around?

Did he take lovers or have a mistress somewhere hidden away?

She covered her face as mortification struck her. She'd given Gideon a present. If he was involved with another woman, she should not have done it. Jessica would not like another woman to give her particular gentleman, if she ever had one, so personal a gift.

And why was it that the moment she'd gone away, he'd formed an attachment to another woman? He was hiding his real nature from her. Pretending to be proper when he must be anything but. There was no reason she couldn't know about his—she swallowed a lump in her throat—*affections* for a woman, unless he still considered her a child who must be shielded from the truth.

She crossed her arms over her chest and glared at the far wall. Jessica had rarely had cause to be displeased with her neighbor, but she was well and genuinely offended. She had told him her deepest, darkest secrets for years, and he never had. She had thought Gideon was a true friend. Friends confided in each other. Well, apparently they were not the friends she'd once imagined.

She turned toward her plants, intent on wiping away dust from their leaves to make them glossy again.

The first pot she pulled toward her sent a splash of water tumbling down the front of her gown. "Oh, no!" she cried, attempting to dab at the spots with her handkerchief. Unfortunately, the little lacy scrap made little difference.

But then she noticed the soil of each plant in front of her was drenched, too. She tilted each pot to drain the excess water then quickly moved each to an empty dry bench. "How could this have happened?"

"Is something the matter?"

She almost jumped out of her skin in shock and spun around. "Mr. Whitfield! Oh, you scared me."

Giddy was the last person she expected to see today, and her face grew hot. She glanced at his mouth, at the lips that had kissed someone else that morning, then turned away. "What are you doing here?"

"I hope you don't mind my interruption," he murmured. "I noticed your water tank had run dry when I came to collect my coat earlier. I've returned to top it up and will be gone in a moment."

Given he was carrying a full bucket of water on the end of each arm, she had to believe his reason for coming was sincere. He had not come to see her, and that thought entirely depressed her spirits. "It was filled only yesterday."

"Well, its empty now," he assured her.

She looked at the rest of her plants and saw all were soaking wet. Too much water was not healthy for greenhouse plants. She tapped the side of the cistern, heard the emptiness within and sagged in defeat. "I must have not shut off the valve properly yesterday."

"I doubt that. Let me have a look." He set the buckets aside and joined her. A series of pipes was supposed to deliver a small amount of water to each pot tray when she turned the valve. It was easier than carrying buckets and much more efficient. But now each dish beneath each pot was full to overflowing.

Giddy squinted at each pipe and then sighed. "Damn. I think it may be broken somewhere."

He turned away, rummaged in his coat pocket and stood with his back to her a long moment. When he turned around, he had spectacles perched on his nose.

Jessica stared at him in surprise. "When did you get those?"

"February."

While she'd been away. She frowned. That was another thing Gideon hadn't yet told her about. Any moment she expected to discover he had become someone else entirely. She would not like that.

She moved toward him and peered up into his face. The spectacles made him seem like a stranger at first, and she had to admit he might be. "You were getting headaches before I left for my season."

He nodded. "Too much reading by poor light at night has strained my eyes, I'm told. The pain disappeared once I started wearing these."

"I'm glad you finally saw someone." She tilted her head to one side, trying to decide if they could still be friends if he kept secrets. If she did not have Giddy... "You look..."

"Even more like my father than I did before," he finished rather glumly.

"You are nothing like him."

"You never met him," Gideon reminded her.

It was true that Jessica had never met Gideon's father, but there was a painting at Quigley Hill of the late Mr. Whitfield. She didn't like it. She'd discovered from listening very carefully over the years that Joseph Whitfield had been as mean-spirited and cold as he'd looked in his portrait.

Gideon was nothing like him. She'd never known him to raise his voice or hand to anyone in anger. "I was going to say more handsome, actually, but I'm sure I'm not the only woman to mention that recently."

"Thank you."

She turned away, blushing, uncomfortable with the knowledge that Gideon had an admirer. She had always liked the way he looked, the way he laughed with her, too. She should have expected other women to learn to appreciate him also.

Jessica avoided looking at Gideon again in favor of draining off the excess water from her plants until her face cooled. "At least now you'll stop squinting at everything and everyone," she grumbled and then shook her head. She hadn't meant to criticize him when she'd missed their conversations so much.

"I wasn't aware I was doing so. My apologies," Gideon murmured.

He started tapping away at the pipework. He bent down on one knee, looking up at the cistern and pipes that spread out from the wall. Jessica paused to watch him, holding back a sigh. He had another life apart from hers—one she might never really know.

"I think there is a crack in the join here," he said. "See?"

Gideon made room for her. She went to him and crouched down so she could see where he pointed underneath the cistern. A tiny bubble of water lingered at the very beginning of the pipework.

"We should summon the blacksmith to have a look at his work," he decided. "I'm sure this is fixable."

"I hope so too," she agreed.

She turned to Gideon, and her breath caught. He was one of her best friends. She couldn't stay angry with him. She wasn't capable of holding a grudge and she'd missed him. But as they remained kneeling very close together, his nearness felt strange—because of the woman he'd kissed that morning, and because he'd avoided kissing Jessica the day before. She thought she'd known him better than anyone.

She hurried to stand up again. "Thank you for your assistance. I'll send word to the blacksmith and ask him to come at his earliest convenience.

Gideon climbed to his feet and then looked around as he removed his eyeglasses. He shoved them into his coat pocket, the same one he'd left behind with her the previous day. "In the meantime, I'll help you clean up."

"I can do it on my own."

"It's no trouble," he promised. "I've no where else to be right now."

She should not have felt relief at his words but she did. If he left, might he go to that other woman again? There was a lot of lifting and sorting to be done. Jessica was not ready to lose him. Not yet. "Thank you. I would appreciate your help very much."

They worked in silence for a while, but Jessica felt the strangeness between them was still there. She could not get past the idea that her neighbor was courting and hadn't said a word about it. Not even to her father it seemed, because Father would have teased Gideon about it already if he'd had the slightest inkling.

She stopped what she was doing and wet her lips. Curiosity curled within her about the stranger. Had *she* been a guest in Gideon's house last night? How long would it be before he proposed? "How was your dinner?"

"Quite good. The roast was perfection, the dining table survived the candles being lit."

Jessica laughed softly, unable to help herself. Giddy always managed to make her laugh, no matter her mood. "Did you banish Mr. Lewis to the stables?"

"Didn't have to. The man refused to assist with anything to do with the dinner."

She stopped what she was doing and glanced at Gideon in surprised. "That's not like him. I've always found him to be very helpful and polite."

Gideon set his hands on the table and rocked forward and back on his feet. "I know. He's been in an odd mood for weeks now. I don't know what's gotten into him. He's become quite surly with me."

She deposited her plant with the others and returned to his side. "Have you asked Mrs. Harrow what the trouble might be? Housekeeper's usually know everyone's business, whether you want it known or not."

"I did ask her about Lewis, but she said she couldn't say."

Jessica tensed as he leaned closer, but then he lifted a large pot, one too heavy for her, and stepped around her. She watched him move the heavy pot to the other side of the room with ease. He returned, brushing dirt off his waistcoat. He was so good to help her. "Couldn't say? That sounds suspiciously like an evasion," Jessica noted.

"That is what I thought, too." Gideon started to chuckle. "When did you get so wise, my lady?"

"I've always been this way, or so Fanny teases me. Fanny says I was born with an old soul." Jessica was proud of that.

"So you were," he agreed, smiling. "But don't forget to leave room to have a little fun now and then."

"I'll never forgot that when I will always have you to remind me," she said, glancing his way. Would he still be her friend if he married? He would certainly have obligations elsewhere then, and if he married this Mrs. Beck, he would acquire sons to raise as his own.

Jessica gulped at that thought. "Mr. Lewis has been at Quigley for as long as I can remember. He is devoted to you and has always been sensible. Whatever the problem is, no doubt it can be solved to everyone's satisfaction."

It wasn't her place to do so but she could involve herself. Mrs. Harrow would probably tell Jessica what ailed Mr. Lewis if she asked the right way.

Gideon approached her. "What are you plotting in that agile brain of yours, my dear girl?"

She smiled sadly. Forever, Gideon would think of her as a mere child. She had grown up, but he couldn't see the change in her. Everyone else had considered her a woman of marriageable age for the last year. Well, everyone but him and her father, apparently. "Never mind, sir."

"You're sad again."

"Am I?"

"I wondered perhaps if you were unhappy with me for not inviting your family to my dinner last night. If I had known you were coming back so early, I certainly would have or changed my plans to another night."

Jessica fought a flush of heat to her skin. "I'm not in despair that I missed out on an invitation. I'm not so childish as that."

"It is quite all right for you to say so if you are."

She sighed and forced a smile to her lips. "I don't expect you to invite my family to every amusement you host, even if they are so very rare."

When he married, their friendship would become less important to him. He wouldn't understand why that saddened her. He would want her to be happy for him. She had to pretend she hadn't seen him kiss that woman and when the engagement was announced, she would also pretend surprise along with everyone else.

"Jess," he said softly. "I can always tell when you're not being truthful, you know."

She shrugged. She should count herself lucky to have had Gideon to herself for so long. She placed her hand on his arm, feeling his strength and warmth through the thin barrier of his linen shirt. Gideon was warm, both in personality and in person. He deserved to be happy, and if that woman made him so, she had to accept the situation. "I'm still tired from the journey and London, perhaps," she promised. "I'm not sure where I belong anymore."

"Your father's marriage has displaced you as mistress of Stapleton Manor."

"I don't mind giving way to Gillian." Jessica leaned against a dry portion of the potting table. "But I will need to find something else to fill my days with. This will not be enough."

He leaned next to her. "What about your little cottage in the village?"

"What about it?"

"It is empty, isn't it?"

"Yes, but...oh, I see where you're going. You think I should empty the cottage of Aunt Grey's furniture, too?"

"That wasn't what I was going to suggest." He nodded. "What do you think of leasing the place, furnished?"

"To whom?"

"To Mrs. Beck."

"No!" The word sprang from her lips without any proper consideration. She turned away from Gideon as her face had grown very hot again. Usually she would listen first, but the thought of that woman meeting Gideon at her own property made her extremely angry.

"Very well. It was just an idea. No matter. I'll find somewhere else for the school."

She whipped around to stare. "School?"

"Hmm, an idea I had. The village hasn't had a tutor living there for a long time and Mrs. Beck is in need of a way to support herself and her sons. I thought setting up a school in the village would be a better location."

She gulped, alarmed at how quickly her temper had spiked for no good reason. "What were the other alternatives?"

"We could always hire the private dining room, but the expense and the noise of patrons might prove an issue. I might have offered the morning room at Quigley Hill as an alternative, but it would be a long walk for any students."

Having Gideon involved with setting up a school would ensure its success—but having him and Mrs. Beck run the place together troubled her.

"Jess, please. Speak your mind to me."

"It's nothing." She had always confided in him, but perhaps it was time to stop because he might not like what she had to say. She smiled quickly. "I should have gone to bed earlier last night. I'm a little tired."

"Talking with Gillian all night again?" Gideon slid one of his arms around her back. It was comforting, but she resisted the urge to turn into his embrace, as she once might have when she'd been younger.

Before the kiss, she wouldn't have thought twice.

Even so, when she breathed in his scent—a combination of the outdoors and the herbal soap Jessica had given him last Christmas—the distance between them seemed to lessen.

He turned her toward him, and then cupped her face between his palms. He stared into her eyes. "Perhaps a lie down will do you some good. With luck, you'll wake refreshed for dinner tonight."

A little overwhelmed by the way he was holding her face so tenderly, she scrambled for her wits. Never before had she hated to ask him a question, and she took a moment before asking the most pressing one. "Do you have plans for dinner?"

"Yes, I'm joining you all." His smile grew. "Your father sent a note about it last night, and I have already accepted."

"Good." She leaned her face into his hand at last but she still wished she hadn't seen him kiss that woman today. She moved back, knowing she must. "Dinners are always more enjoyable with your company. No one in London is ever interested in fungus the way you are."

He laughed heartily at her observation, eyes twinkling with mirth. "I'm glad. Now, about these plants of yours. We'd better get busy saving them, yes?"

"Yes, Giddy." She drank in his smile. "Thank you for helping me."

Chapter Six

————◆————

Gideon sighed. "I see there is no escaping gossip."

The Duke of Stapleton wagged a finger at him and then sat himself down in his usual chair in the Stapleton library. "You should have told me about this yesterday. I wasn't pleased to be the last to know. Napier took great pains to shove the hint in my face when I met him outside the church."

"You did have company yesterday. I could not speak freely," Gideon protested, glancing about the familiar room for anyone lurking about. "And there is nothing to tell."

He'd not actually seen the duke alone since his return to the estate. Revealing his new acquaintance with Mrs. Beck wasn't a pressing issue anyway.

"Tell me more about Mrs. Beck," the duke

pressed. "She'd left the chapel before I heard about her."

"There's not much to tell. Mrs. Beck is a widow, and she's been living with the Napiers since April began."

"Poor woman," Stapleton murmured. "And you've been seen walking out with her."

"Our paths have crossed several times in recent weeks," Gideon corrected. "I'm not courting the woman."

"And yet everyone thinks that you are. You hosted a dinner the other night. She was there, wasn't she? You've only held three dinners, to my memory."

"One for every decade of my adult life," Gideon agreed with a laugh. "I thought it was time to brush off my hosting skills once more. I'm quite rusty; I quickly discovered."

The duke grinned. "Is she pretty?"

"Who?"

Stapleton raised one haughty brow, waiting on an answer. It was a look he used to intimidate many.

Gideon, long used to his habit, laughed instead. "I suppose she is."

"It is past time you married, you know," the duke suggested. "A wife would do you the world of good. So would children."

"That again," he complained. "You know my feelings on the subject."

"Now don't dismiss the notion out of hand again, sir." The duke, rarely one for serious discussion, appeared affronted. "Were you not the one who decided I should marry again and played a hand in matching me with my Gillian?"

Gideon grinned widely. "It seemed the best and most honorable solution, given the way you were mooning over her night and day."

The duke pulled a face. "I was not mooning. I was admiring with restraint," he said with great indignation. "I would have gotten around to pursuing her eventually," he grumbled.

"After Jessica had children of her own, no doubt." Curiosity about Jessica's time away in London grew in him. She was not happy, and so very little had been said about Jessica's first season or her suitors.

The duke shrugged. "I'd like to see her settled with a family of her own, and children too."

"That would be best," Gideon agreed, but the idea of Jessica moving away had always unsettled him. Jessica was special; he'd always believed that. She needed a good man as her husband. Someone who would look after her, protect her and the children they made together.

As if summoned by his thoughts, he spotted Jessica standing just outside the library. She glared at him so angrily, he blinked in surprise.

The duke swiveled around in his seat. "Ah, Jessica," the duke called. "Was there something you needed?"

"No." She wet her lips, and then smiled so normally, he wondered why she hid her feelings from her father. "Can I come in?"

The duke sighed. "For a little while but only if you help me tease Gideon."

She moved into the room and sat in a straight-backed chair between them, facing the fire. "Why would I do that?"

"Because Mr. Whitfield may not remain a bachelor after all."

"Of course I will." But Gideon shifted in his chair, uncomfortable that Jessica be involved in any discussion about Mrs. Beck. It was not proper to discuss his love life, or lack thereof, with her in the room. Considering the appeal of one woman over another was something he did not do around her.

The duke rose to take his glass and refill it at the sideboard, and he took the opportunity to set the matter straight. "I'm not courting anyone," he whispered.

Jessica, a high color in her cheeks, shook her head. "But you *are* kissing someone," she whispered back, her eyes accusing.

His eyes widened, and he had no response to give. Had Jessica been spying on him? The cheek of the girl!

Her eyes dropped, demure once more as her father returned. The subject of Mrs. Beck was thankfully dropped in favor of more amusing topics but the damage was done. Jessica did not believe him. She'd seen them and would not take his word at face value.

"Are you interested in a visit to Rafferty's tomorrow, sir?" The duke asked. "We thought to take the Garlands on a tour of the district."

Jessica cleared her throat. "I asked Mama if I might remain behind, but she said I must ask you for permission."

"You don't want to come to Rafferty's with us? But you loved trying your hand at fishing last year."

"I liked it but I was younger then, Papa," she chided. "If I stay behind tomorrow, there will be more room in the carriage, and the boys will not have to share fishing poles."

"There could be fewer squabbles that way, too," Gideon added, hoping to be helpful and supportive of Jessica's wishes. "Unfortunately, I have other plans for tomorrow, too."

Children enjoyed fishing a great deal, and while Jessica had excelled at the sport, perhaps she had outgrown the desire to participate in rough pastimes.

"That's a shame." Stapleton moved across the room and dropped a kiss to Jessica's forehead. "I sometimes forget that you're all grown up now."

"There is a lot of that going around," she grumbled softly.

Stapleton sat, looking at his daughter with surprise written all over his face. "Oh?"

She looked at her father steadily for a long time. "Pretty soon, I won't be the youngest anymore."

Stapleton sighed. "She told you?"

Jessica looked at her father with a disappointed expression. "She didn't have to. I can read the signs as well as any woman."

Gideon looked between them. "What is this?"

The duke smiled slowly. "Apparently, I'm to be a father again. I hadn't expected, not at our age, but…"

Gideon burst to his feet and shook the duke's hand vigorously. "My God! Congratulations, my friend. Congratulations indeed."

The duke seemed to be blushing though as he accepted Gideon's congratulations. "It's early days yet. Best to keep it quiet for now."

"Father, the household staff already know," Jessica warned him. "They were plumping every pillow when Gillian came down this morning and offering to fetch her anything she needed. You should have told me yourself. Neither of you thought much of me."

The duke appeared suitably abashed. "Ah, sorry, pet. We thought, with your season and all, that it might be best to wait to share the news after you'd made your choice. We didn't want to influence your decision."

Jessica stood suddenly. "A baby does change things. Gillian shouldn't return to London, so we're not going back this year."

The duke gaped, but Gideon understood instantly. Jessica thought more of Gillian's comfort than her own ambitions for a husband. The trip back to London would be tiring for a pregnant woman and the rigors of the season an added strain. As far as he knew, Gillian had never had a child. Her first, at her age, might be a delicate time.

He was so proud that Jessica's first thought was for the comfort and welfare of the new mother.

"We thought perhaps Fanny might consent to chaperone you for the rest of the season," the duke suggested.

Jessica's expression grew outraged. "No! I'm not leaving Gillian. She's not been well and might need my help to manage Stapleton later."

Her father appeared stunned. "Don't you want to return to London?"

"Yes, one day but not now. Not this year." She glanced toward Gideon and away quickly. "If you'll excuse me, I'll leave you two gentlemen to do what you usually do at night."

"Good night, sweetheart," the duke said as she swept out of the room.

Jessica paused just outside the door and looked back at Gideon when he said good night, too. He knew that expression well. She wanted to talk to him in private. Tonight.

When she turned in the direction of the long gallery, he guessed where he'd find her when he was free. She'd once waited for hours just to ask him to explain a joke that had gone completely over her head.

"She's upset," the duke murmured.

"But not about the baby," Gideon noted, setting his drink aside.

"No, not about that." The duke frowned. "I always thought the next child I held might be hers."

Gideon tipped his head back against the chair, imagining Jessica holding her own babe. She would make a good mother. She was kind and sweet and playful. Her husband would be a lucky man.

He glanced across at the duke. "You never said either way, but was there no one she favored in London?"

"Not that we ever noticed. Truth be told, Jessica seemed disappointed in her season. I fear it was a mistake to bring her out."

"It wasn't a mistake. When Jessica is ready

for a husband, we'll all know it."

The duke smiled. "Sometimes I forget how well you understand my daughter. You're always the first to suggest patience and speak up on her behalf."

"Years of steering her away from trouble," Gideon added.

"You are the brother she should have had."

"Brother?" He snorted. "I softened the snubs her siblings caused. They were always too busy to include her, too important to play and answer her questions."

"But not you."

"I suppose not, but I don't think of her as a sister," he said, chuckling at the thought. He was an only child. Glad of it, too, since any siblings he might have had were spared the experience of his father's harsh punishments. Despite the problems Stapleton's offspring had caused, the duke had never harmed them. The Westfall children had experienced a gentler upbringing than Gideon had ever known was possible.

The duke looked at him with an odd expression. "How do you think of her?"

"A friend," he was quick to clarify.

The duke grunted. "I was hoping you'd say that."

"Why?" But then he suddenly knew exactly what the duke was about to suggest.

"With the duchess increasing, I want to stay close to my wife as much as I can. Jessica will need someone to watch over her when I'm busy elsewhere."

Gideon didn't find the idea disagreeable. He'd been protecting her since she'd been old enough to crawl into fireplaces. "You can count on me to keep an eye on her."

The duke's smile was immediate. "Thank you. Now if you would excuse me, I'd like to find out if my wife has managed to keep her dinner down tonight. I'll return in a little while."

"Take your time." As soon as the duke departed, Gideon jumped out of his chair and went in search of Jessica. He found her not in the long gallery, but outside it in the garden, staring up at the stars.

"There you are," he murmured quietly. "What are you doing out here alone?"

"Did Father ask you to convince me to stay with Fanny in London? You can save your breath. I shan't be going anywhere."

She'd been listening for a while then. Gideon was not unduly alarmed by that. Jessica had always liked to know what her father talked about. "We didn't speak about the matter of your season again. But he wants me to keep an eye out for scoundrels who might take advantage of you while he stays close to Gillian."

She laughed softly. "All the scoundrels were left behind in London."

"Oh, there might be a few lurking about in the countryside still. You never know when they'll make an appearance," he teased. "Why else did you set me to dog Miss Hawthorne's steps while you were away?"

She turned slowly, her expression unreadable. "Are you one of them? A scoundrel."

"Me? Good God, no! Why would you ask such a thing?"

"You lied to Papa. You *are* having an affair with that woman. Mrs. Beck."

Gideon reeled that she would be so blunt. It did not sound like Jessica was pleased that he might be courting, either. Jessica hadn't much exposure to the romantic side of adult life, but she was his friend, and idealistic. She may have thought a single kiss meant he really was enthralled. "It is not an affair."

She shrugged.

"It is not."

She put one hand on her hip and glared at him. "Then why did you kiss her?"

"She kissed *me*, and I hope she will not do so again."

"I heard all men want women to kiss them."

"Some do, I suppose." He raked his fingers through his hair, feeling uncomfortable with the topic. "It was unexpected. I hope to remain friends with her."

"Friends?"

"Allies is perhaps a better term." He sighed, knowing he must reveal a little about Mrs. Beck's situation. "Do not spread this about, but she likes the peace of Quigley Hill and her boys like that there are few rules. She's been here less than a month, and her brother-in-law has already suggested she's a burden on his household and to consider marrying again."

"You feel sorry for her?"

"She's not had an easy life, or will not have, being entirely dependent on Mr. and Mrs. Napier's dubious support."

Jessica frowned. "But you do admire her?"

"Only enough to wish her an easier future. The school was my suggestion, a way she might be mistress of her own home again. I have been very clear about my views on marriage, so she cannot mistake my offer of assistance as romantic in nature."

Jessica's frown cleared and she looked up at him. "Well, if you are not courting her, I would like to ask for your help, too."

"Of course, anything."

She wrung her hands. "I let Natalia believe that I had been kissed in London, and she will want to talk about it when she returns for luncheon tomorrow. Help me! I can't very well describe something I've never experienced."

He almost laughed but when her words sank in, he sobered very quickly. Gentleman should have been lining up to capture her. Kiss her. He'd expected that. "Surely that cannot be true?"

Her head dipped even more as she nodded.

Oh, it was always bad when she dipped her head that low. "But you were courted?"

"My dowry was," she whispered, turning away.

He grabbed her shoulders and turned her back to face him. He made her look up by slipping his finger under her chin and lifting it. "Jess?"

"I'm so humiliated."

"I'm so sorry." But Gideon's temper rose. Trust those fortune-hunting noblemen to spoil her season. He was offended on her behalf. "You'll have to lie to Natalia, or tell her the truth."

"You know I'm no good at lying and the truth is too horrible to repeat again." She turned away, brushing at her cheeks. "I want you to kiss me so that I might save face. I cannot be the only young woman in the district who hasn't been kissed! I've had a season in London, and I'm not going back this year. It's expected that I'm more experienced than I am."

She lifted her big beautiful eyes to him, and

his usually sane heart urged him to agree to her request. His mind, however, controlled his tongue. "No."

"Please, Giddy! I'd be forever in your debt. It's either you or ask Charles Henderson."

"The hell you will!" He nearly shook her but made himself release her and calm down. "Your father would skin the Henderson boy alive if he touched one hair on your head, and then he'd lock you up in your room forever."

"So you do it. He wouldn't hurt you. Or perhaps you could just agree to let *me* kiss *you*." She sighed softly. "I'd much rather make a fool of myself with you than anyone else. No one needs to know."

"I'll know." But dear God, he was in trouble, judging by the look of determination in her eyes. He'd seen that expression on her face too many times to easily dismiss her request. It wasn't a whim, and she wouldn't forget. She might ask someone else to do it the moment his back was turned too. "This is a bad idea."

"No, it is not. I know you wouldn't want to trick me into marrying you if we did. You've made your feelings about that very clear."

He considered his options. He should refuse…but to have her kissed by a local man, someone coarse who might force her to wed them, wasn't the least bit palatable.

Or Gideon could kiss her *his way*, which

could never lead to marriage.

He glanced around to make sure they were still alone and then held out his hand, palm up. "Remove your glove."

"What?"

"Just do it, or I'll leave you right now."

"But…"

There was an adorable crease between her brows, and he hardened his heart against doing what she'd really asked for. When her hand was bare, he gently cupped the back of it with his, holding hers palm up. "Close your eyes."

She did, and then her chin lifted, and her pink lips pouted toward him.

Ignoring her mouth, Gideon worked his own glove from his fingers with his teeth and shoved it in his pocket. He looked down at Jessica's hand laying so perfectly still in his grip. She had delicate fingers; pale, almost translucent skin. She was soft in all the ways a woman born to wealth should be. Jessica had never known a day of hardship in her life, and he was determined to keep it that way.

Using one fingertip, he lightly brushed her inner wrist, and then softly stroked her skin toward her palm. Her fingers twitched at his touch, and the frown returned in full force.

She kept her eyes closed but a soft gasp left her lips as he continued to taunt her skin. He smiled at her reaction. He enjoyed teasing her.

He valued each and every response to his caresses. He was determined to make this the best almost-kiss of her life.

He smiled as he drew his finger lightly down the length of each of hers, until he could hear and see the effect he had on Jessica's breathing.

He studied her face for each precious change in her mood, catching her biting her bottom lip to hold in her response. He drew a little closer as he began to draw circles on her sensitive palm. A tiny whimper escaped her control, and he grinned widely. He had never imagined seeing Jessica warm to any seduction of his...but she was enjoying this.

He tapped the center of her palm and then closed her fingers into a fist. He held her clenched fist a moment before drawing back from her.

Jessica's eyes flashed open. Her lips were parted, and a shuddering sigh left her lips.

He took another step back, pleased with her reaction. He pulled his glove from his pocket and tugged it back on.

Jessica drew closer, fist clenched around her own glove. "You cheated me out of a proper kiss."

He hid a smile. "Perhaps, but that should be enough to help you fool Miss Hawthorne."

"Miss Hawthorne?"

He glanced at her face. Her cheeks had reddened, and her lower lip was plump and pink from biting it. Had he completely muddled her with just his touch? Remarkable. "You said you needed Miss Hawthorne to believe you'd been kissed before? That is what it feels like. Mostly."

She stared at him, and then her eyes widened. "Truly?"

"Would I lie to you about something so important?"

"I hope not but…"

"Think of how it felt…not knowing what would happen, the disappointment when I stopped. A good kiss should always leave you wanting more."

Her brows furrowed. "Do you?"

"Of course not."

He returned inside without looking back, trusting Jessica to return indoors in her own good time.

Chapter Seven

———◆———

Jessica was glad of the peace and tranquility of her home, a much-needed reprieve from her last months in London.

As she restyled her hair for the afternoon into a simple bun with a few pins, she thanked the stars for Gideon. She felt calmer now; confident in a way she'd never been in London. For months, she'd despaired of her new situation as a woman in search of a husband. Despite all the advice offered, it wasn't until she'd experienced her first taste of intimacy with Gideon that she understood why anyone would want to marry.

His touch, a cunning pretense of kissing her, on Sunday night had bolstered her confidence with barely any effort. "My first kiss was lovely. Everything you said it should be and more," she promised Natalia, who had called that afternoon. Given the sweetness of the moments she'd spent alone with Gideon, she was now happy to talk about her experience in glowing terms.

Natalia laughed softly then leaned close. "Isn't it strange that having a man's tongue in your mouth can actually feel lovely."

Jessica murmured her agreement, although she hadn't a clue tongues could be involved. Gideon hadn't said anything about that. Maybe the next time they met, he could be persuaded to further her education a little more. She still yearned for a real kiss.

Natalia helped herself to a second cup of tea. "So it seems your Giddy and Mrs. Beck are still causing tongues to wag in the village today."

Jessica stared at Natalia in shock. "What?"

Natalia wrinkled her nose. "Mrs. Napier called on Mother this morning and all but announced a wedding."

"No." Jessica couldn't believe her ears. "Giddy swore he wasn't pursuing Mrs. Beck."

"I saw them, too, standing outside that little cottage you've inherited." Natalia's eyebrows rose high. "Did you really ask him if he was courting her?"

"Well. Yes." She fidgeted, and then clenched her fingers together to control her agitation. "He said he was being kind, helping Mrs. Beck feel at home in new surroundings."

Jessica made no mention of Gideon wanting Mrs. Beck to run a school from her own property. She couldn't fathom why they had been looking at her cottage when she'd been very clear she wouldn't lease it to the woman.

"That is not how Mrs. Napier puts it. I definitely heard the words 'smitten' and 'inseparable'." Natalia leaned forward. "Do you think he is hiding his interest in her from you?"

That was troubling. His interest in beginning a school might lead people to believe he was pursuing Mrs. Beck, no matter what he said to the contrary. And with Mrs. Napier stirring the pot and believing a match might yet be made, the pair would continue to be gossiped about.

"He wouldn't deceive me about something so important. It's not true."

Natalia sighed. "Good. Frankly, I don't care for the woman. I like Mr. Whitfield, and I'd hate her to snare the most eligible bachelor in the district. Everyone, and I mean *everyone*, has tried to catch his eye at one time or another. Some still try even after they've married, I heard, too," Natalia warned with a laugh.

A little ball of worry formed in the pit of Jessica's stomach. As long as Gideon remained a bachelor, unmarried women would pursue him. The thought didn't settle well with Jessica. "He is popular, isn't he?"

"Indeed. An excellent dance partner and quite amusing when he's not driving off any would-be suitors he doesn't approve of. I vow, he's more intimidating than my father ever could be if he were inclined to try it." Natalia scrambled to her feet suddenly and peered out the window. Jessica's room overlooked the front drive. "Oh look. There are three carriages headed to the manor!"

"Father only took one out today."

"I think he is the one leading the procession." Natalia turned to face Jessica, her face growing pale. "They are moving very slowly. I do hope nothing went wrong today on their outing."

"Mother!" Jessica flew from the room and down the staircases with her heart in her mouth. Mama hadn't been completely well for some time but had insisted she was well enough for a short journey. They were so much earlier returning from the outing to Lord Rafferty's estate than she'd expected that it could only be bad news.

Imagining the worst, Jessica rushed outside to wait on the front steps. Natalia was a little slower, catching up a few minutes later.

Jessica remained on the uppermost step as the family carriage finally paused at the bottom, wringing her hands. The Garlands tumbled out promptly, the children telling her of the fish they'd caught that day. But her father and mother took their time exiting the carriage.

Unable to wait a moment longer, Jessica rushed to the door and poked her head inside. "What happened?"

Father scowled fiercely. "Your sister is coming—and she brought acquaintances from London. Met them in the village after fishing."

"Rebecca? Again?"

"Now, not a word about Gillian's condition to anyone."

Natalia gasped, and father heard her. He wagged a finger at Jessica's friend, too. "Your lips are to be sealed while Mrs. Warner is in residence as well."

"Yes, your grace," Natalia promised, stepping back to allow Jessica's parents to exit. "Not a word."

Gillian came close once she was on her feet in the fresh air. Despite the dreadful news, she seemed happy enough. "You missed a wonderful day out, my dear."

"I'm glad you all had fun without me," Jessica murmured, forcing her anxiety to dissipate.

Gillian looked over her shoulder, her smile slipping. "I did, and now we must be on our best behavior. Our unexpected guests are almost here."

Jessica looked too. The carriages were just

entering the turning circle of the gravel drive. "Who is in the other carriage?"

"Lord Newfield and his son, Lord James," Mother said sourly.

"What?!"

"I thought you said Lord James was soon to be engaged?" Natalia whispered in Jessica's ear.

"Everyone expected it." Jessica shrugged. Lord Newfield was here to talk to Father most likely about politics, so he would be no trouble, but Lord James...she'd no idea why he'd come. "I hate how Rebecca always arrives without warning. She hasn't lived here for a decade."

"So does his grace. I need to shake off the dust and change before I face everyone."

Jessica hooked her arm through her mother's. "I'll come with you."

"Perhaps I should go home now," Natalia murmured. "Mrs. Warner doesn't really like me."

"You are always welcome, my dear," Gillian promised. "Your presence might stop his grace from venting his spleen."

"Oh." Natalia paled. "No, I think I should definitely go home."

She dipped a quick curtsy and quickly fled down the path that led to the boundary with the village. Jessica watched her go with a pang of regret. "I wish I could do that."

"So do I, my dear. So do I."

They spent an hour above-stairs while

Gillian changed her clothes and talked about her outing. Jessica eyed the slight tummy her new mother had developed with growing fondness and a touch of exasperation. A new sibling wasn't exactly what she'd hoped for when her father had married her companion, but she was pleased for them. A little worried about her, too. Mother seemed tired nearly all the time but insisted she was well enough to face their guests at last.

Jessica wasn't looking forward to the next few days. Rebecca had been quite against Father's decision to remarry and had avoided speaking to Mother while they had all been in London. Rebecca thought Gillian beneath their family and could not see how happy Father had been made by marriage.

Not that he'd been miserable before. Father found amusement everywhere, consorting with a large group of friends, including Gideon Whitfield, and had enjoyed his life. But he'd needed someone to come home to. Someone to share the ups and downs of his life with. Gillian fit that need perfectly.

Rebecca couldn't have come home at a worse time for the couple. Father was tense with worry over the pregnancy already. Having Rebecca looking down her nose at Gillian for her humbler origins would only make him more cross. And with Lord Newfield and his son here, too, pushing his political agenda, there would be little peace and quiet for the newlyweds. "Should we wait for Mr. and Mrs. Garland?"

"My brother and his wife wish to spend the afternoon with their children," Gillian murmured. "Pony rides have been arranged."

"Half their luck!"

"They go home tomorrow, and I do hope their last night is not spoiled."

"I won't allow that," Jessica promised. "We should invite Gideon for dinner. He is a wonderful distraction."

"Unfortunately, I already know he has other plans for his evening," Mother sighed. "We will have to make do without him tonight."

They descended the stairs together and at the doorway to the drawing room, Jessica allowed her new mother to move just ahead of her. She was determined to show her support for this marriage any way she could. Gillian was the Duchess of Stapleton, and it was high time Rebecca accepted her elevation, as far as Jessica was concerned.

Even the butler seemed to sense the mood and played his part, announcing the duchess' arrival to the duke and Rebecca with a great deal of pomp when it wasn't strictly necessary with only family present.

Father, of course, did what he always did.

He strode across the room, took his wife in his arms and kissed her soundly, regardless of who was watching. "All right, darling?" he whispered to Gillian.

Mother nodded and smiled. "I am now."

Rebecca smiled only at Jessica. "At last."

Mother and Father turned at the sound of her voice, Mother's hand resting lightly on Father's arm, and stared at Rebecca, who remained at a distance.

Jessica's sister drew near, her expression almost pained, and dipped a shallow curtsey. "Your grace."

"Mrs. Warner," Mother began. "What brings you to our home at this time of year?"

Rebecca's smile was a fragile thing that never reached her eyes. "I felt the need to be with my family."

Mother nodded. "I see? Well, we are happy to have you back."

Rebecca's nodded. "Thank you."

Mother smiled serenely. "Please, won't you sit down?"

There was a moment when Rebecca's chin trembled, but she sank down without another word. Father caught Gillian's hand in his. "Mrs. Warner wishes to remain with us for the summer."

"Lovely," mother murmured, but Jessica was struck by Father's odd tone. Rebecca was never at Stapleton for the whole of summer. Usually, she remained in London or flitted about the countryside visiting her friends. By the way Rebecca was twisting her fingers in her lap, Jessica suspected that something was wrong.

Rebecca had married young and been widowed the same. Granted a generous independence within her settlement, she'd lived mostly in their brother's townhouse in London—at least until she felt people needed reminding that she was a duke's daughter.

"Lord Newfield and Lord James," the butler announced suddenly.

Jessica turned to view both men as they swept into the room.

She inclined her head as greetings were exchanged but stared at Lord James, trying to figure out what he was doing in the countryside—*her* countryside in particular—without his soon-to-be bride. Lord Newfield and his son were similar in looks. The father rounder, the son thinner. Both had thick, unruly hair in a dull shade of brown. She could easily see how Lord James would age just by looking at his father now.

Jessica eased toward her sister to whisper, "Rebecca, why did you bring them here?"

"I did not." Mrs. Warner closed her eyes briefly. "But stand straight and smile. They are both too important to offend."

Jessica was heartily sick of hearing that she had to be agreeable to every stuffy bore who wanted a moment of her father's time. When Lord Newfield engaged Father in conversation about the latest debate in parliament, and mother and Rebecca began whispering together, Jessica found herself more or less alone in the son's company.

Lord James bowed deeply to her. "Lady Jessica! How well you look today."

"My lord."

She did not like that he would just turn up unannounced and uninvited.

Lord Newfield returned. "London is not the same without your beauty to brighten up the ballrooms, is it, son?"

"What rubbish," she muttered under her breath. Lord James had never noticed her when she'd been in London. He'd had his eye on another woman. She looked directly at him now. "I trust you left Lady Hannah in good health."

A flicker of surprise showed in Lord James' expression. His jaw firmed, and he seemed to almost shake his head. "I expect she is well," he said softly.

But maybe not happy? Determined to give Lord James no encouragement, she turned to his father. "Lord Newfield, I heard you were needed in parliament for the debates still."

"Indeed I am." The marquess nodded. "Your

sister mentioned the jewel of the family had returned to the country unexpectedly soon, depriving the marriage mart of the finest debutant."

Jessica's stomach turned over at that ridiculous statement. "I see."

"My son is not one to give up the hunt so quickly," Lord Newfield announced.

It was hard to mistake his meaning. When Lord James said nothing to deny it, she took a tiny step back and planned to make more.

Lord James smiled in her general direction but his gaze flittered around the room. "It is good to return to Stapleton Manor."

"I thought so too." *Until now.*

He frowned. "I very much enjoyed the Christmas I spent here with you."

"With my family. There were a great many others present, too."

"Yes, it is indeed good to be here. I should have liked to have met you before the season had begun," Lord Newfield promised, slapping his son on the shoulder. She heard the air whoosh from Lord James' lungs as if it were her own. She felt exposed and desperate to escape them.

Jessica forced herself to stand firm. "Yes, I had thought coming home a good idea too, once," she repeated. "It is usually so peaceful."

Lord James winced.

However, Lord Newfield beamed, missing

her meaning entirely. "We look forward to seeing more of the beauty Stapleton has to offer."

Jessica could not say the same anymore. She had hoped she'd left the marriage mart and the fortune hunters behind. But here was Lord James, acting as if Lady Hannah had never existed. She never imagined he would follow her home. Oh, she wished they hadn't come, that she could turn tail and run into the gardens right now. But appearances mattered, even at home, as did not giving offense to men her father needed the support of in the House of Lords.

She stood in awkward silence for a moment, and then Lord James asked if she might like to take a walk in the garden together.

"I've spent most of the morning in the gardens," she informed him quickly. "It's a busy time of year for the estate."

"I'm sure it must be," he agreed. "So what new sights might I see on this visit?"

"Everything is different since your last visit. There is no snow to cover up the real beauty of Stapleton." She smiled suddenly, remembering Gideon's advice last winter. "But of course, you must have come to study how Stapleton's famous mushrooms grow in the warmer season."

"Mushrooms again?" he muttered under his breath.

Bless Giddy. The mushroom conversations Jessica had started with her unwanted suitors in London bored almost everyone to tears. Lord James had already suffered through several different conversations about fungus. It was his own fault if he must endure another. "Oh yes, the gentry come from miles around just to learn how they are propagated, so it is not as great a secret as it should be."

"Propagation of mushrooms. Isn't it enough to simply have the servants pick them from the fields?"

"Oh, no. The farming of mushrooms is so much more complex than that." She nodded enthusiastically and smiled, determined to drive Lord James away. She didn't care if he thought her completely dotty. That was part of her plan too.

His smile faltered a little. "Perhaps you would teach me about mushrooms and about the gardens while I am here."

"Oh, well, you do not need me for that. Most of the responsibility for the garden falls to Father's land steward. You need to speak to him for specifics, but he's occupied elsewhere for the rest of the day, unfortunately." Jessica tapped her chin, considering how best to get rid of Lord James quickly. People frequently came to Papa for advice. Perhaps talking of the estate instead of politics with Lord Newfield would cool Papa's temper over Rebecca's sudden visit, too. "If you would come with me. Father is the next best person to help you."

Without waiting for a response, Jessica marched across the room and inserted herself into the conversation with her parents and Rebecca. "Excuse me, Father. Lord James is most interested in the estate and in seeing the gardens today, particularly the extensive kitchen gardens, where our fungus grows. Can you help him?"

"Oh, yes," Mother murmured. "I think that a fine idea."

Father stared at Gillian, and Jessica was sure some unspoken communication was taking place because his lips twitched. Rather than feel excluded, Jessica was grateful. Mother could always convince Father quicker than anyone she'd ever met. It must be because they loved each other.

"Yes, of course," Father agreed, nodding slowly. "Come along, Lord James. Lord Newfield, you should come too. There is much to see on your *short* visit with us."

Jessica suppressed a smile. Short visit? How smart of Father to set limits on their stay with just a few words.

Father took Lord James and his father away.

"I came as soon as I realized Lord Newfield was planning to follow Father into the country," Rebecca blurted out as soon as they were gone.

Gillian sighed. "The bill will never pass in its current form. Your father had told Lord Newfield that long before we left."

Rebecca winced and glanced toward Jessica. "I don't believe that is the only reason Lord Newfield has come."

"Why has he then?"

But Jessica knew the reason already. "They have come for me. For my fortune, more precisely."

"Indeed. Our paths crossed in London, and Newfield peppered me with questions about Jessica. I fear he has driven his son here to ask Father for your hand in marriage on his son's behalf."

"That is my impression, too." Jessica scowled. "But Lord James is all but engaged to Lady Hannah Alexander, or he seemed about to be."

"But his father still holds the purse strings, so he may not have a choice in who he weds." Rebecca winced "And he is a powerful ally for Father. He tends to get his own way in everything, too," Rebecca warned in a quiet voice that sent shivers over Jessica's body.

"I will refuse Lord James, should he ask," Jessica promised. "I'm not marrying someone who treats me the way he has Lady Hannah. I don't care how important his father thinks he is. I won't marry a fortune hunter. Not ever."

Rebecca sigh suggested relief. "I suspected that, which is why I wanted to be here to advise you. When you refuse him, it must be done with great delicacy."

Gillian enveloped Jessica in a hug, mothering her in a way she'd become used to in recent months. "Having my brother's family around tonight might delay Lord Newfield from discussing his intentions with your father. I had no idea about Lord James' renewed interest in you, neither did your father, I'm sure. I'll warn him as soon as I can."

"We'll handle this as we do all unpleasantness," Rebecca promised. She took a deep breath and let it out slowly. "As a family."

Jessica tensed, but Gillian only nodded. "We'd better amend my request for tea, don't you think, my dears? Jessica, could you find Brown and inform him that tea will be needed for only the three of us. I think we'd best retire upstairs to my private boudoir, where we can talk freely and not be disturbed."

Family. Jessica was grateful for all the help she could get, especially if it brought Mother and Rebecca closer. She pulled them both into a hug. "Thank you."

Chapter Eight

———◆———

Gideon rubbed the moisture from his hair and his body, glad the grit was gone from his skin. Building a bathing room at Quigley had been a costly though useful addition, especially for a single man with only a few servants.

Without a large household staff, the effort of bathing had become a much simpler chore since the installation of a boiler for piping water to this tiled room. Having warm water running from pipework instead of lugging bucket after bucket from the kitchen saved everyone's backs from the burden, too.

He usually didn't bathe so early in the day, but an accident that had seen him slide on a muddy field had made being cleaner highly desirable.

He slipped on the banyan he'd been given a few days ago for his birthday and grinned as the fabric encased his body in such soft delight. The luxury of the garment and Jessica's generosity still overwhelmed him when he put it on each day. He could never repay Jessica for the gift, so he made sure that each wear wasn't ever taken for granted.

It was his own fault he'd fallen rather than paying attention to where he'd placed his feet. He'd been daydreaming—as he'd done too often since Sunday night's encounter with Jessica.

Foolishness.

He buttoned himself up so he was decently covered for the dash upstairs to his bedchamber to redress in clothes suitable for the outing he'd decided to make that afternoon. He was expected at the tavern soon. The proprietor had hinted he might be interested in the regular coin to be gained by hosting the school, at least for a little while.

Unfortunately, he had made no progress in finding Mrs. Beck and her sons other accommodation this week. Their safety concerned him more and more each day. No matter the time they spent away from the Napiers' residence, Mrs. Beck's spirits continued to decline, too.

Glancing at himself in the full-length mirror, he felt he looked satisfactory for a man closer to old age than his youth. He felt younger today, especially so after he'd tricked Jessica into believing a kiss felt as good as his touch.

Teasing her with that hint of seduction had been more fun than it ever should have been.

He shook his head at the direction his thoughts had traveled yet again and exited the bathing room, head down, steps light on the boards so he wouldn't draw the attention of his female staff who were lurking about—always ready to make teasing remarks about his latest mishap. Cook and the housekeeper sometimes giggled and whispered, which made him decidedly uncomfortable.

"Hello, Giddy," Jessica whispered out of nowhere.

He spun around in a circle, clutching his robe tight to his chest.

However, the hallway was empty. He'd only imagined her voice.

"Over here," she whispered again, and he realized the sound came from a nearby storeroom.

Jessica *was* here.

Gideon glanced around quickly, but he was entirely alone in the hall. Drawn by the appearance of her beckoning hand from the darkness within, he crept toward the room as silently as he could and found Jessica waiting among the preserves. "What are you doing?"

"Running away from home," she whispered before grabbing his arm and tugging him fully into the storeroom with her.

She closed the door slightly, giving them privacy but leaving enough light so they could see each other once his eyes adjusted.

Jessica looked lovely. Fresh. Smiling. Extremely pretty in a soft yellow muslin gown.

And he…was in a robe with nothing on underneath.

His face warmed with acute embarrassment. "What the devil, Jessica? You cannot just hide in my storeroom."

Her smile slipped away. "I needed an escape. Rebecca arrived on Monday afternoon."

"I heard a whisper she was back." He didn't exactly blame her for this escape. Rebecca was well on her way to becoming a shrew from all he'd heard and seen in recent years. "I suppose I'd hide from her, too, if we were related, but still, surely there were other places you could go besides here. What about the attics at home? Miss Hawthorne's?"

"I like it here better," she confessed shyly. "Mother was still abed and feeling poorly again, and Father has been dragging Lord Newfield and Lord James about the estate since dawn each day. You'd know that if you'd called on us."

Gideon ignored the reprimand. "Lord James has returned?"

"Unfortunately, yes." She shrugged. "I couldn't bear another morning of hiding from him, so Mrs. Brown and I concocted a plan to visit your staff."

"I see." He glanced toward the door, hoping not to see Stapleton Manor's housekeeper next.

When he looked toward Jessica again, her attention had drifted downward to his feet as she took in his improper appearance, but then she looked up, smiling. "I'm glad to know you are wearing my gift. You really do look very well in it."

"It is much warmer than my last one. Thank you again." He was *quite* warm, despite being nearly naked. "You must leave, Jessica."

Before her reputation was irreparably damaged by their proximity. Scandalous was putting it mildly.

"But I am still discussing housekeeping matters with Cook and Mrs. Harrow."

"Housekeeping? Of my home?"

"Sort of." She drew closer, and her voice dropped low. "I found this delightful little shop in London. The scent of the spices was incredible when I passed by, so I went in and purchased a few of them to experiment with. Mother's stomach is too delicate for strong scents right now, and I couldn't wait, so we came here to discuss the best use of them with your staff."

At least Jessica had a fair excuse for visiting a bachelor's household. She'd brought a chaperone with her, too, which was an excellent decision and would protect her reputation. "Are you planning to make more soap again?"

"Possibly," she murmured. She leaned even closer, resting her hands on Gideon's upper arms, and obviously inhaled him. "That's the one we made for you last Christmas, isn't it?"

To his shock, his cock thickened beneath his robe beyond his power to stop it. *Hell!*

"I suppose it must be," he whispered, face burning with shame and shock. This should not be happening to him. Not with her.

Jessica continued talking, unaware of his inner struggle. "We have decided that most of the spices would be best served with food, and were just coming up with possibilities for a menu. You'll be there to sample them all, of course."

He gulped. "I can't wait."

"Lady Jessica?" his housekeeper called. "Are you there?"

Gideon quickly covered Jessica's mouth so she didn't make a sound. "She can't know I'm with you dressed like this," he whispered into her ear, and then moved to stand in the shadow of the door.

Once adequately hidden, Jessica poked her head out into the hall. "Yes, Mrs. Harrow."

"Did you find what you were looking for? Do you need any assistance?"

"No, I have everything I need right here." Her hand waved about toward him, and he caught her fingers before she knocked anything from a shelf. "I'll return in a moment."

She nudged the door nearly shut again and linked her fingers through his. "I need that jar of peaches in ginger wine and the treacle jar behind you," she whispered.

He looked over his shoulder without a clue where any of those items might be. He needed his reading glasses for anything written down, but he'd left them in his study down the hall. He could not leave this room in his current state.

Jessica released him and stepped close. She wrapped her delicate fingers around the items she wanted while he tried in vain to rid himself of his erection. Jessica moved them to an empty shelf by the door and returned. She looked up into his face and smiled again. "I haven't seen you in days. Come for dinner tonight."

He should refuse, but to his shock, he nodded instead. By tonight he'd have his body under control. At least he hoped so. "I am free tonight."

"Perhaps tonight we might talk again, and after dinner you can show me what a real kiss feels like."

He gulped. That was partly why he'd stayed away since Sunday. He *knew* the way Jessica's mind worked. She was always eager to learn and rarely forgot. "Not a good idea."

"Your last lesson in kisses did me no harm." She searched his face. "Thank you for that, Gideon. Natalia was completely fooled by my description of your kiss."

"I'm glad. Jess…" he whispered. "Listen, I need to get dressed."

"Do you?" she asked, eyes widening as she appraised him.

Dear God, she'd learned how to flirt while she'd been away. He wasn't having it. She was too close, lips rising to his.

He reared back.

Jessica pouted and dropped to her heels. "I was only going to say goodbye."

"It is not a good idea to tempt a man not wearing trousers," he warned.

Jessica's eyes danced with amusement. "I've seen your bare legs before when you go fishing with Papa, Gideon. They're not that shocking."

She hadn't seen higher up than his knees, and higher than that was precisely where his problem was currently making itself obvious. He leaned forward a little more, making sure his banyan draped loosely about his hips, and gestured to the door impatiently. "Go back to the kitchen so I can get away without being seen."

Jessica looked him up and down again, brow furrowing. He grabbed her by the shoulders and shoved her toward the door. "Go."

Jessica laughed softly, one hand gripping the door latch. Light streamed around her body like a halo. She was beautiful and beguiling— and thoughts usually ignored seeped into his consciousness as clear as day.

She was a woman now. Of an age to be a wife. A lover.

He was a bachelor. An old, delusional one, perhaps, but still a man with normal desires.

He wanted to kiss her very badly.

He clenched his jaw over a curse that would shock her and shook his head. "Leave now."

She sighed somewhat happily and collected the jars she'd come for. "Don't be late for dinner. Lord James is a tedious man, and I've already discussed the growing of mushrooms twice with him already."

He smiled despite his discomfort, and Jessica slipped away smiling, too. His amusement died the moment she was gone.

He shut the door, leaned against it and thumped his head against the wood once. What the devil was wrong with him! He should not feel this way about Jessica. It was an aberration, brought on by his state of undress. He turned about and faced the dark room. *Bollocks. I'm only human.*

And she is very pretty, persistent, and hardly ever worried about propriety around you.

He pinched the bridge of his nose in a bid to get himself under control. He thought of the school and the good he hoped to do for Mrs. Beck. He and Jessica were friends and neighbors. He would act as if today had not happened.

He looked down and frowned.

He would as soon as he had *that* under control.

———◆———

Was it fair that Jessica had to always wait forever when she wanted to talk to Gideon? No, it was not. Jessica drummed her fingers on the old tabletop, ignoring her third cup of tea. She felt the restrictions of her status as an unmarried woman most keenly today.

"These are lovely," Mrs. Mills gushed, inhaling the subtle fragrances of the spices Jessica had purchased in London.

"Indeed. Very subtle," the Stapleton housekeeper agreed.

Mrs. Harrow glanced toward Jessica. "Something on your mind, my lady?"

"No. Not really," she promised. But the warmth of the kitchen was making her mind wander. Too much more and she'd fall asleep right in this chair. She couldn't sleep here. This wasn't her home.

But it could be, her wayward imagination suggested.

She sat up a little straighter, watching as the servants divided up the spoils of her London shopping trip between them.

As they worked and debated, she kept one ear cocked for the sounds of Gideon moving about. Unfortunately, his bedchamber was located one floor up and on the other side of the house from where she currently sat. But she suspected she would hear Gideon on the stairs when he came back down after dressing.

She laid her hand against her throat. She had not minded seeing him the way she'd discovered him today, and ever since, well, the urge to surprise him again appealed tremendously.

Now she knew something very personal about him, even if it must remain a secret. That made her feel decidedly smug. Opportunities for catching Gideon unawares, however, had never come about very often. She toyed with two little bowls of spice before her. "Would you combine these two?"

Mrs. Mills shook her head, but Mrs. Brown nodded. "In shaving soap, perhaps, with honey to smooth the scent. His grace's former valet concocted something very similar once I think. But that was years ago now. He did not leave behind his recipe."

"That is a shame." She could imagine this scent on Giddy's skin. She fought a blush and drew those spices toward herself. "I'll keep these for now."

Mrs. Harrow beamed. "They will last until you've a husband to use them for. Perhaps Mrs. Brown could have another look for that recipe in the meantime."

A husband? Was there nowhere Jessica could go that did not include a discussion of her future marriage? Now she was back in the countryside, she'd rather not think of the future—the children she was supposed to want, the husband she was meant to please. The fortune hunter dogging her steps.

She much preferred talking with her friends. Teasing Giddy, too.

She glanced over her shoulder. He seemed to be taking a very long time to change and return downstairs. Had she missed hearing him? Had he slipped away to call on Mrs. Beck without saying goodbye? She glanced at his staff, curious about the way he really conducted his affairs when she was not around. "I understand Mr. Whitfield hosted a dinner recently."

"Aye, he did. A successful affair it turned

out to be."

Mrs. Mills clucked her tongue. "Well, it would have been if not for—"

"Shh," Mrs. Harrow hissed, glancing at Jessica and Mrs. Brown guiltily.

Jessica looked between the women. "What are you not telling me?"

"I'm sure it's nothing," Mrs. Harrow promised.

"Not nothing. I've got my suspicions." Mrs. Mills crossed her arms over her ample breasts.

"About what? Is this about Mr. Lewis behaving strangely toward Mr. Whitfield?"

Mrs. Mills shook her head. "He sees what's going on, too."

Jessica sat back in her chair, annoyed with them for dangling such a tiny scrap of information before her and not explaining. "Well if you're going to remain cryptic about the matter, I think it's time to take my leave."

The pair protested, but Jessica stood anyway. She scooped up her shawl and draped it around her shoulders. "Ladies, thank you for a pleasant afternoon. Don't get up. I shall see myself out."

"It's that new woman, the one living with the Napiers," Mrs. Mills blurted out.

"Hush," Mrs. Harrow warned.

Jessica turned back slowly. "Mrs. Beck?"

Mrs. Mills nodded even though Mrs.

Harrow said nothing.

"What has she done?"

"She's got her eye on him."

The only gentleman Mrs. Mills and Mrs. Harrow had ever worried about was their own master. "On Mr. Whitfield?" she asked, just to be sure she had the right of it.

"Yes," both said in unison.

"I don't believe you've anything to worry about. He's always said he would never marry."

"Because of the way his father was with him," Mrs. Mills grumbled. "Too hard on the boy, he once was."

All the air released from Jessica's lungs. She knew very little of Gideon's life before her birth, but now that she considered it, Gideon never spoke of his father or with any sadness that he had passed away. Jessica sank into a chair slowly, ready to listen to the two women who might know more about Gideon than anyone alive. "Tell me."

Mrs. Mills picked up a rag and scrubbed at a spot on the tabletop. "Punished unfairly, he was. Over nothing but some imagined slights. His mother was too timid. Afraid of her husband."

"And now Mrs. Beck's boys suffer the same tyranny under another's hand," Mrs. Harrow whispered, leaning toward Jessica. "It would stop, of course, if he married the mother. He's a gentle man, our master. We fear he would do anything to spare a child so much pain again."

Jessica gulped. She could easily see where the ladies' imaginations were heading with this. "He's a good man."

"He'd be a good husband. A kind father if he but trusted himself not to turn out like him."

Was that why he'd vowed not to wed? Why she'd never heard a whisper about Gideon courting until now? Jessica would never believe Gideon could be cruel, and she was about to say so, too, but she heard a heavy tread on the staircase and shushed the ladies quickly. She began to discuss the spices again as Gideon's familiar steps slowly drew near.

Chapter Nine

———— • ————

Gideon walked heavily toward the housekeeper's chamber to announce his impending arrival. He could hear Jessica's voice in the room and he did not want to disturb them. However, he did not pay his servants to sit around drinking tea all day with his neighbor's youngest daughter.

He brushed his fingers along the familiar walls of his home as Jessica made gentle suggestions for improvements to his menu as if she were mistress of the house.

It always amazed him how concerned Jessica was for the comfort of others, but it wasn't right that she fussed over him.

He headed into the kitchens and all conversation stopped. He looked about the room and inhaled the strong scents of Jessica's purchases. "Forgive the interruption."

Mrs. Harrow smiled. "What can I do for you, Mr. Whitfield?"

"Nothing. I was just on my way out."

His cook started to get up. "We had just finished. Time to start your dinner anyway."

"I'm dining out tonight."

Mrs. Mills sat down with an obvious sound of displeasure. "Again?" she grumbled softly, although everyone in the room would have heard her.

"Dinner will be the usual time, Mr. Whitfield," Jessica said quickly.

"You're dining at Stapleton tonight?" Mrs. Harrow exclaimed. "I'll let Mr. Lewis know to brush off your best suit early so you'll not be late."

Jessica rose to her feet. "I am on my way out now, too, so that is excellent timing."

Jessica collected her bonnet from a hallstand while he stood watching. His arousal had thankfully subsided but his memory of it had not. "I'll see you out then," he suggested.

He waved to his housekeeper and gestured for Jessica to precede him outside. He would help her climb into his carriage and see her safely headed for home with her chaperone.

Gideon set his hat on his head as the Stapleton housekeeper joined them. "It's a lovely day for a carriage ride, my lady."

Jessica grinned. "Perfect, actually, but I

think I should like to walk home instead of taking the carriage."

Jessica was an energetic woman, and impulsive, too. He worried for her chaperone, who was getting on in years. "What of Mrs. Brown? Will you make her walk home, too?"

"Oh, no. I'll send her back in the carriage with Mr. Lewis, if I may borrow him for an hour to drive her. Do you mind going home without me very much, Mrs. Brown?"

"Of course not, my lady. I know how you like to stretch your legs." The housekeeper smiled warmly. "I'm sure Mr. Whitfield will see you safely home."

Even when it wasn't proper? After the events of today, it was even more wrong. However, the Stapleton housekeeper seemed to find nothing wrong with Jessica's plan, and he was very puzzled by her agreement. "She is always safe with me," he promised.

The housekeeper smiled warmly. "Good."

Gideon saw Mr. Lewis on the far side of the garden, and when called for, Lewis was quite happy to comply with his request. He doffed his hat to Jessica and even smiled at Gideon, too, for the first time in weeks. Lewis promised to bring the carriage to Mrs. Brown if she would but wait a few minutes in the shade.

Gideon and Jessica left the housekeeper behind on a bench. He put his hands behind his back as they walked along. "Strange that. Mr. Lewis must be over his mopes at last."

"I hope so, too," Jessica murmured as she suddenly claimed his arm. "I have missed our walks."

He had, too. Perhaps he should follow behind at a distance. However, she'd said Lord James had returned, and he could be loitering in the garden in the hopes of catching her alone. He would not like her to be surprised by the appearance of a fortune hunter while she was unguarded.

They moved beyond the first enclosure, taking the usual path toward her father's estate. Jessica, wearing a sunny smile and full of excitement, glanced about happily. "How far shall we walk today?"

"You are walking directly home, young lady."

She pouted. "There's nothing improper about us walking about Stapleton together, and I need to talk to you. In private."

"Oh?"

She rubbed her brow. "Giddy, I have a problem I can see no easy way to deal with."

"There is no problem you cannot overcome, Jessica. You are a sensible, intelligent young woman. You know there is nothing that can stop you once you make up your mind. What is the problem, and we will figure out what to do about it?"

She stopped under the shade of an oak and rested her fingers on the trunk, remaining silent a painfully long time. "Rebecca says Lord James has likely come to propose a marriage between us, and I think she is right."

He looked at her sharply. "You don't like the idea?"

She looked at him and blinked. "Giddy, he's so boring, and was obviously in love with someone else just last week. I saw him with Lady Hannah Alexander in London. I thought, like everyone else, they were in love. I never expected to see him here!"

"He's from a powerful family."

"His father is wealthy and a bully, I think. Lord James has pockets to let and depends on his father for his living. I suspect Lord Newfield has dragged him here to propose to me simply because he's desperate for a large dowry and the connection to my father. Lady Hannah has only a small dowry, but her father is not so well liked. If Lord James' desperation made him in any way attractive as a marriage prospect, I'd never feel this eager to escape my own home. Rebecca says I must refuse him the right way without offending his father, but I worry just saying so once will not be enough."

He looked at her in surprise. "Rebecca supports your decision to refuse him?"

She nodded. "On this, she and Mother are

on the same side—mine. But nothing they've said so far gives me hope that this will not cause consequences for Father later."

He rubbed his hand across his mouth. "Short of being already engaged, I can only suggest being honest with Lord James. If he's in love with another lady, as you believe, then he is probably equally unhappy to be here now. As a gentleman, he must accept your decision without argument."

"But as a member of parliament, his father may find a way to punish *my* father later in some devious way."

"You don't like Lord Newfield at all, do you?" She was wise to fear parental manipulation. "What does your father say to do?"

She looked up at him. "Father says he loves me, and it is my choice who I wed. I just never thought my decision could affect him."

He brushed his fingers from her shoulder to her elbow, wishing there was something he could do to ease her fears. "It shouldn't be like this for you."

"That is why I desperately need you at dinner tonight. I can't fake another megrim for the third evening in a row."

"Do you want me to monopolize Lord James' attention for you?"

"You managed that very well at Christmas

without me even asking you to," she noted.

"I wasn't aware I'd been so obvious."

"Oh, I noticed, and I did not mind at all."

Gideon had been justified at Christmas—Jessica hadn't been out, and her father had wished for his involvement in keeping an eye on Lord James. "A bachelor with no interest in marriage has his uses."

Her fingers landed on his arm. "I might need even more help than just having you step between Lord James and I tonight. I fear he's actually becoming interested in our conversations about fungus now. He's asking all kinds of questions that test my knowledge of the subject!"

"Well, that is inconvenient." He considered what to do. Many lords were in need of funds and an heir, and the simplest way to remedy the shortfall was to marry a young lady with a large dowry from an impeccable family.

And Jessica had a dowry of twenty thousand pounds.

A clever man could do a lot with that level of funds at their disposal. An *ambitious* man could bribe the servants to look the other way and ensure Jessica had no choice in the matter of who she wed. He did not like to think Stapleton's servants were so mercenary, but it wasn't unheard of when there was a lot of money involved. The first time could be more than enough to land Jessica in a scandal she couldn't escape.

Gideon stared across the garden, jaw clenching. He had always hoped Jessica would be pursued by someone who loved her. "Perhaps I could be of use—with the right incentive."

"What sort of incentive?" Her gaze flashed to his, mischief shining brightly in her eyes. "I could pay you in kisses? Real ones, and not that clever trick you did with your finger on my palm."

He shook his head. He'd walked directly into that trap all by himself. "How about you play the pianoforte after dinner instead? I haven't heard you since Christmas. I have missed the sound."

She nodded, but it was apparent his answer had disappointed her. "Then I will play for you all night if it keeps Lord James at bay. No duets. What would you like to hear?"

He smiled. "Any music that makes you happy."

She smiled back. "I'll play just for you then. I know your favorites by heart."

"Done." He would enjoy that—the music *and* thwarting a rival for her affections. He tried to lead her toward Stapleton Manor, but as had happened before, Jessica resisted and turned the other way.

"Jessica, where are you going?" He pointed in the direction she should be going. "Home is that way, or have you forgotten."

"Please don't make me go back yet. I will be cooped up with Lord James soon enough. I just want to walk a while more with you."

Reluctantly, he nodded. Those odd desires he'd experienced earlier had not returned. Jessica was safe, and he wanted to put the troubling moment firmly in the past. He pointed to the path that would bring them back to Stapleton manor in a roundabout manner, past fields where Stapleton's servants always toiled.

They would be seen together every step of the way.

Jessica stopped to speak to several of the oldest fellows, enquiring what they were doing and how they had been while she was away in London. There was a new man on the estate, and she asked the land steward to introduce them.

Gideon was not happy about that when he got a look at the great hulking fellow. The new man was young and obviously strong, arms and legs like tree trunks, and he towered over Jessica. And over Gideon, too, for that matter.

When the fellow looked upon Jessica with a lusty eye, that set Gideon's teeth even more on edge. "Lady Jessica," he said, raising his voice to interrupt. "You are expected back at the manor."

"So I am. Goodbye, Mr. Sweet. We'll talk again soon."

Mr. Sweet? Ridiculous name. The damn man looked dangerous, especially around Jessica.

She rejoined him quickly enough but after a few steps, she looked back over her shoulder. "Goodness, he *was* impressive, wasn't he?"

He looked back over his shoulder at the sweaty young man staring after Jessica like a hungry beast. He pinned the man with his darkest scowl until the fellow had the sense to look away. "Hard to tell under all that mud."

"Strong, too." Jessica chuckled. "The maids have been talking about the new man nonstop. I had to see for myself."

Gideon stopped and his scowl returned, only this time directed at Jessica. He definitely didn't like the idea that she was admiring the servants on her father's estate. "If you dare say you fancy him…"

Instead of being chastened, Jessica gaped at him—and then doubled over and peeled with laughter. He stood awkwardly until she recovered, wiping her eyes. "Never in a thousand years, Giddy."

Apparently, he'd completely lost his mind today and overreacted yet again. "Forgive me."

"Mr. Sweet has a sister living with an aunt in the next village. The aunt hasn't very much to live on, and the girl is of an age to take up a position. To begin to learn about her potential, I needed an introduction. He's the head of the family and responsible for her. I'm hardly likely to fall into a swoon over someone I just met like the silly maids have done."

Chastened, he looked away. "I should hope not."

Jessica laughed again and clutched Gideon's arm. "Giddy, there are days when I think you know me better than I do myself, and others when you don't know me at all."

Gideon walked on a few steps in silence, Jessica's arm firmly curled about his. "About your suitor?"

"Lord James isn't a suitor I want, Giddy. When I came home, it was with the assumption that I had none."

"That's ridiculous." Gideon anticipated that Jessica would release him soon, but she moved her hand along his arm, fingertips pausing at the inside of his wrist. They danced lightly over his pulse in the most maddening way. He stared down at where she touched him and gulped back a moan. "I'm sure you will not remain unmarried for long. When you return to London next year, who knows who you will meet then."

"Did you ever doubt your decision not to marry, or did you always want to live alone?"

"I never really thought about it."

Jessica squeezed his wrist and sighed. "You could change your mind."

They were veering into territory he'd rather not speak of. He shook his head quickly. "I won't. Not now."

Jessica pressed her cheek against his shoulder suddenly, like she had when she'd been a child and scared during a thunderstorm. "I missed you," she whispered.

Gideon bit his tongue rather than admit he'd missed her, too. He untangled himself from her grip regretfully—before Stapleton Manor appeared through the trees and anyone saw them nearly embracing.

Just as well he had, too. The duke was walking the gardens, speaking with a stranger just ahead. Lord James trailed behind, snapping off the heads of flowers while no one stopped him. "Is that Lord Newfield with your father?"

Jessica slid behind him as if trying to hide. "Yes."

Gideon studied the gentleman strutting along at Stapleton's side carefully. Older than himself, slightly portly with a booming voice that carried across the grounds. He turned his attention back to Lord James following behind. The young man slouched and displayed none of the bravado he had at Christmas. At Christmas, Lord James had exuded confidence as if he owned the world.

Perhaps his father was the one who *owned* him.

If that were the case, Lord Newfield was not a man Jessica should ever be related to. When they all stepped into one of the walled gardens surrounding the manor and disappeared, he turned to her. "I'll escort you directly to the doors."

She nodded. "Thank you. I'm glad you're here. After you go home, I am going to remain upstairs in my room until you return at dinnertime. I'm not giving them a chance to catch me alone tonight."

Gideon inhaled sharply. "Are you that afraid of them?"

"No." She shrugged. "Well, perhaps a little, but only in that if they say he wants to marry me, I am going to refuse on the spot. That would be awkward."

"I won't let Lord James corner you tonight." He had no right to get involved, but he certainly could make a nuisance of himself. Title or not, money or not, Jessica deserved to be pursued for who she was, not how much money she might bring to any marriage.

Chapter Ten

———◆———

There was something so right in having those
she loved most gathered together at Stapleton.
Jessica was seated in her usual place at her
father's table, Gideon on her right, Rebecca
seated opposite. Mama and Papa were next to
each other at the end of the table, whispering as
they often did. They proved that friendship and
marriage went together so well.

Jessica was proud that they ignored the
London trend. So many married couples there
barely spoke to each other in public. That was
the sort of marriage she had already vowed not
to have. When she wed, it would not be just for
her dowry. She wanted what her father had
found with Gillian. She wanted to be loved.

Father had invited a few local families to
join them tonight. The Hawthornes were there,
as were the Forsters and Georges. All

neighbors who shared a border with them, actually. And Gideon had kept his word and had never been very far away since his arrival. She was having the most marvelous time and enjoying her conversations with him immensely. They had talked of mutual acquaintances, Gideon's plans for his garden, and the projected yield rates for the fungus grown at Stapleton Manor—but only whenever Lord James was near.

Now, the dinner was drawing to a close. He would be gone soon.

Lord James, seated on her left, cleared his throat. "I wondered if you might join me tomorrow for a carriage ride to the village. His grace has suggested horses but—"

"A horse ride is a lovely idea. Will everyone join us for a ride to the river tomorrow?" she asked, looking around the table. "We could have a picnic."

"As long as the journey is not begun before dawn." Lord Rafferty, a distant neighbor, shrugged. "My cook likes to sleep late."

It was Lord Rafferty who liked to sleep late. Although he was gruff and at times off-putting, Jessica quite liked the earl. He was a good friend of Gideon's, and her father's, too. He always blamed his servants for his tardiness, which no one ever really believed.

"I think we can accommodate your cook, my

lord. Perhaps we could meet at eleven if that's not too early?"

She heard Lord James mutter "perfect." She smiled but didn't dare look in his direction. Jessica would make sure to be busy until eleven.

Lord Rafferty sat forward suddenly. "I have a better idea. Mr. Whitfield, are you of a mind to race against me again?"

Rebecca stiffened. "Foolishness. You'll break your neck."

Lord Rafferty downed the contents of his wineglass and gestured a servant to refill it again while Rebecca looked on with a sour expression. He looked at the wine and then to Gideon. "Well?"

"Oh, yes, do," Jessica begged, turning to Gideon in excitement. The last race had been a source of great entertainment for the estates they rode near. Jessica had not been permitted to race herself, nor did she feel the need to do so, now she was older, but she'd be present for the start and glorious finish when Giddy won.

Giddy smiled her way quickly before he addressed their neighbor. "First round the borders wins a crate of Rafferty's finest wine for their table?"

Lord Rafferty nodded, a fierce light in his eyes. "First to the finish wins a barrel of Quigley Hill Ale. We start and finish from the front drive of your estate, Mr. Whitfield."

Gideon nodded. "Done."

"Well, my son shall amuse the ladies and keep them out of harm's way in your absence," Lord Newfield announced importantly without asking them their opinion.

Jessica glanced across the table as Rebecca sucked in a sharp breath, just as annoyed by that suggestion as she was. Lord Newfield clearly thought women could not amuse themselves. Another good reason to refuse the son, should he propose.

Lord Rafferty glanced at Rebecca and smirked. "Care to make a wager on the outcome, madam, or would you care to race against us?"

"Don't be ridiculous," Rebecca said primly. "I've better things to do with my time than challenge a pair of foolish men."

"Suit yourself. Lady Jessica?"

"She will not be racing either," Rebecca tossed out. "We've no need to compete with any man."

Rebecca's eyes flashed with anger, primarily directed at Lord Rafferty.

Jessica made a show of considering the matter, and then nodded. "I will watch. And I will gladly place a wager on the outcome," she informed Lord Rafferty.

She had always cheered for Gideon. She had no doubts about his commitment or skills in the saddle.

However, what she wagered would need to be spelled out now, and she'd already spent her pin money on Gideon. "The winner may have the pleasure of escorting me to the next ball."

Beside her, Gideon began to choke. "Getting Rafferty to a ball is no small undertaking. He rather famously does not dance, either."

She glanced at Giddy and smiled serenely. "Then perhaps you had better make sure you win, Mr. Whitfield, so you might have the pleasure of dancing with me instead."

Everyone at the table laughed and began to place wagers on the outcome, too. Gideon's brows lifted in surprise at her words, but she wouldn't retract the challenge. She would dance all night with Gideon if it were allowed. He'd never once stepped on her toes. In fact, when they had danced together, Jessica had often felt she was floating in his arms.

Rebecca excused herself from the table suddenly. Mother excused herself, too, and followed Rebecca into the hall. When her father departed as well a few moments later, Jessica knew it was her responsibility to lead the conversation at the table until their return.

She turned back to those remaining, seeing friends but also two adversaries surrounding her.

Lord Rafferty was staring at Jessica when

she looked at him. His gaze flickered to Whitfield and back. "That was a very bold suggestion, my lady."

Jessica lifted her chin. "Was it?"

"Quite." Lord Rafferty brows lifted. "I would prefer something very particular, should I engage in a wager with you, Lady Jessica."

Jessica stared at him without blinking. But her heart began to thump against her breast. What if he asked for something scandalous? She would of course refuse, but it might be...awkward.

Lord Rafferty pursed his lips. "If I beat Whitfield to the finish, I want..." His eyes glittered briefly. "You, to visit Rafferty Park the next day."

She blinked. "I beg your pardon?"

"Out of the question," Gideon growled out as he threw his napkin onto the table. His expression was harder than she'd ever seen it. His leg pressed against hers under the table when she went to speak, most likely to elicit her silence. His warmth seeped through her gown at the knee, and she warmed all over instantly. "You go too far, Rafferty," he warned.

She turned to Lord Rafferty though. It always shocked her when people she'd known for years suddenly forgot their manners when her father was away from sight. Visiting Lord Rafferty was not something she'd ever want to do.

She smiled even as the pressure against her leg increased.

She could of course count on Giddy to defend her from a scoundrel, but she did not need his help with Lord Rafferty. If she wanted to be considered a respectable woman, she had to stand on her own feet when faced with such a bold invitation. "I would love to spend an hour visiting your daughter."

The earl stared, eyes glittering fiercely again. But then he laughed. "Yes, of course. What other purpose could I mean?"

Gideon's leg retreated from hers, and she missed the connection to him almost immediately.

Jessica let her breath out and settled her hands in her lap. "As everyone here must know, I adore children, and I am curious about your offspring. My father and mother will be happy to escort me, I'm sure."

Lord Rafferty barked out a laugh. "A wise answer, my lady."

Beside her, Gideon let out another soft exhalation as he returned his napkin to his lap. "Nicely done," he murmured softly.

Warmed by his praise, Jessica smiled at those gathered still at the table. They began talking amongst themselves almost immediately. With everyone distracted, Jessica slipped her hand across to Gideon's where it rested on his thigh, and she traced her fingers over his knuckles very lightly. "Thank you."

He jerked his fingers away from hers.

She sighed and faced those at the table. "If you gentlemen will excuse us, I think it's time for the ladies to take tea. Mr. Whitfield, might I depend on you to satisfy my father's guests in his absence?"

"You may," Gideon said. "A word first, if I might be indulged."

Jessica stood, and the ladies rose, too, chattering as they headed across the hall for the drawing room and the tea that was already arranged to be offered there. She stopped by the door, in a spill of candlelight but in full view of everyone. "What is it?"

Her heartbeat quickened as he drew closer. "I suggest you not bait Rafferty, Jess. He's every inch a scoundrel."

"Obviously. A man who refuses to rise early is not to be trusted." She frowned though. "He's Father's friend. He's harmless."

Gideon made an odd sound, stepping closer until Jessica felt warm all over. "Friendships are different between men than between men and women. Remember, you are a woman he could ruin. Be cautious in what you say to him in the future, please. Visiting his daughter was not what he was going to suggest. The next wager might just be for your virtue. Trust me, he would not marry you to hush up any scandal, no matter who your father is."

Jessica smiled up at Gideon's dear face, noting the worry he couldn't hide tonight. There was no chance she'd give herself unwisely. She knew her own mind, and Jessica knew now how far a lady should trust a gentlemen. "I'm not a fool."

"I know." He frowned, expression turning more serious by the minute. "It's just...you know it can be easy to become swept up in the moment and go too far."

Was that what he thought was happening between them? She glanced toward the great hall where they'd been alone, so oddly passionate and yet wholly chaste, and then back to his face. She hadn't been swept away when she'd asked Gideon to kiss her. She was as rational about her neighbor as she'd ever been. She liked him. She trusted Gideon implicitly. She'd always wished him to be closer. But apparently, he was not comfortable with that idea and, thanks to his staff, she knew why that might be. Or did he still think of her as a child? She longed to show him how grown up she could be. "Did you see how bright the stars were tonight?"

"I did when I walked over." He glanced out the nearest window. "Looks like I will have starlight to walk home by, too."

"It must be lovely to do that. Go anywhere you like, when you like, without anyone telling you what you do."

She smiled as she formulated a rather daring plan for later that evening that would show him how she had changed. Jessica twisted her fingers together at her waist to hide her excitement from him. Gideon had a terrible habit of anticipating her actions and putting a stop to them. She'd once thought he could read her mind. If he read her mind now, he might be somewhat shocked by the direction of her thoughts.

"I suppose that's one way to look at it. Jess?"

She smiled at him brightly. Everything had to change between them—starting tonight. "Yes?"

"Whatever you're planning is a bad idea."

She grinned. "I know what I'm doing, Giddy."

His eyes bored into hers. "I don't think so."

"Oh, yes I do." And tonight was only the beginning of challenging the status quo with him. "I had better go. Mama will expect me to entertain her guests until she returns."

She hurried to the drawing room before he could argue or pry into her plans.

The difficulty, of course, would be leaving the house undetected. If the guests lingered too long over drinks or Gideon departed early, she might miss him entirely. And Mama sometimes checked on her after she'd gotten into bed for the night. She would have to chance that she wouldn't tonight.

When Gillian finally arrived in the drawing room, appearing happy and content, Jessica made her way to her sister's side to lay the groundwork for her later escape. "Is everything all right, sister? You've been so quiet on this visit."

"I am always quiet."

Given she had left the dinner table early, Jessica could not really believe her. "Why do you always lie to me when you are upset?"

"I am not upset," she insisted. "Mind your own business."

Rebecca was definitely hiding something. For a change, Rebecca had not been harping on about marriage and potential suitors too much. In fact, Rebecca was offering all sorts of advice to repel gentlemen like Lord James. "I'm old enough to know what is really going on," she murmured. "You can trust me not to tattle. I never would do anything to embarrass you."

"You're not the one who could embarrass the family." Rebecca turned to Jessica. "What do you think of Lord James now?"

"My opinion has not changed."

"Yes, that much is obvious. You barely paid Lord James any attention when he spoke to you at dinner. Have you told anyone else our suspicions about why he is here?"

"Only Mr. Whitfield."

Her eyes narrowed. "Whitfield?"

"He's been most helpful in the past," Jessica rushed to explain. "I trust him."

"Do not be fooled. Whitfield is a man, much like Rafferty and his ilk."

"Gideon and Lord Rafferty couldn't be more different," Jessica protested. "I know you don't like Lord Rafferty very much, but don't you dare tar Gideon with the same brush. He's my friend."

Rebecca stiffened. "You could have smiled more while you were in London."

Jessica sighed, annoyed she'd have to defend herself yet again. "I wasn't happy there."

"Happiness is fleeting and friends are never as they seem." Rebecca looked around the room and wet her lips. "You'll come to understand that soon enough."

"Well, I'm happy now, and I'm going to make my own decisions about who and when I marry."

Rebecca shook her head. "You could still make an advantageous match if you tried a little harder."

"I have done my best," Jessica grumbled. "I do not want to marry a fortune hunter. I want someone who desperately wants *me*."

She'd never been in a hurry to marry, although everyone else seemed to be. She wanted someone who could not wait to be with her. A man who valued her mind and opinions. A man who would make an effort to understand her. A man who could teach her about passion and desire and real kisses.

"You sound like Fanny," Rebecca chided.

At that moment, the gentlemen strolled into the drawing room in a mob, talking amongst themselves about tomorrow's challenge. Her eyes lingered on Gideon, and she yearned to rush across the room to join him, to hear what he had to say about his chances. She thought too about his fingers on her palm, and she tingled all over again when she remembered their recent conversations.

Gideon was a man who knew about passion and desire and real kisses, even if he never wanted to be a husband. And Jessica wanted Gideon to kiss her so very much.

Jessica moistened her lips as she studied Rebecca with fresh eyes. Her sister had never seemed happy with her life, and she'd married for prestige if not a title. Jessica wanted more for her life than that. "I think Fanny had the right idea, to marry for love and never settle for less. She said the only reason men sought her out before and after she was widowed was to take her fortune off her hands. I want to be loved."

Rebecca frowned. "Love is not easy to find or keep, sister."

"Well, I'm young and patient," she promised. "I'm not in a hurry. I'll wait for the right husband to notice me."

When Gideon moved toward her, she made room for him. He took the hint and squeezed in beside her on the settee. The warmth of his body resting briefly against hers, the scent of his cologne, filled her with a happy warmth. But when Jessica looked around from greeting him, Lord James was scowling at her.

She raised one brow at the fortune hunter, daring him to go away. Thankfully he took the hint. He tossed back his drink and then stalked off without saying good night to anyone.

With her unwanted suitor gone, Jessica leaned her body a little closer to Gideon's. Now she could really enjoy herself at last.

Chapter Eleven

———— ✦ ————

Dinners at Stapleton usually left Gideon in a happy mood. Good food, excellent wine and the conversation of intelligent friends to round out the occasion. Tonight, however, the wine had not appealed, and his friend had disappointed him beyond a shadow of a doubt.

The idea that Lord Rafferty would turn his amorous gaze on Jessica made him angry and more than a little worried. Jessica was too trusting. He was afraid that, despite her words to the contrary, she would not be strong enough to reject Rafferty should he seriously pursue her.

He slapped his hat against his thigh as he walked along toward his home in the moonlight. What he wanted to do was turn around and lock Jessica in her room to protect her from all scoundrels—men like himself, too.

He couldn't forget he could have kissed her, but he must do so soon for the sake of his own sanity.

Pining for what he shouldn't want, what he must deny himself, would drive him mad.

He stopped and silently berated himself. That gown Jessica had worn tonight...damn, he should not be thinking about the way the soft fabric had clung to her curves. Rafferty and Lord James had been ogling her cleavage all night, too.

Their interest made him sick to his stomach.

Both men held titles; only Rafferty was genuinely wealthy, but Lord James' father was powerful. Both men had merit as potential suitors, he supposed. Rafferty might marry Jessica if he let himself fall in love with her. Lord James would marry her for her dowry alone.

But any man could love Jessica if they spent more than a minute in her company, besides considering the enormous size of her dowry and connections.

"The stars are lovely tonight, aren't they, Gideon?"

Gideon let out an oath and turned around. Standing in the shadows of a nearby tree was Jessica. She was alone, dressed as she'd been for dinner, stunning him yet again by her sudden appearance. "Devil take it! How long have you been standing there?"

"A while." She smiled without any hint of embarrassment or contrition. "I knew you would walk this way home. You are as much a creature of habit as I am."

"Then we had better change our habits if we are that predictable." He glanced back at Stapleton Manor. They were far enough away not to be seen, thank heavens, but their voices might carry on the night air. "Predictable undoubtedly makes a gentleman dull company," he confessed in a whisper.

"There is nothing dull about you, Giddy. I like you exactly as you are," she promised in an equally low voice. "If you were less predictable, I'd have the devil of a time catching you unawares."

He glanced at her again and noticed her smile had widened. "Why would you want to catch me?"

"It's always been fun surprising you." She drew closer and grinned. "I don't get to do it very often. You're always so careful to observe the proprieties, too. Don't you ever get tired of always being proper, always making sure that nothing we do or say can get us into trouble?"

He frowned. Keeping Jessica out of harms way was becoming a full-time occupation. Her father would be furious to know she was traipsing around the gardens alone in the dead of night. It was after midnight! "You shouldn't be out here alone."

"I'm not alone. I'm with you." She moved closer still, looking up at him with a pleased expression. "And I am undoubtedly safer with you than in there. Lord James is prowling the house. I think he might even be inebriated."

He grabbed her arm, but Jessica wasn't so safe with him wearing that dress. Not now, that much was certain. She was close enough to capture. To kiss. All he'd have to do is lean forward and their lips would touch.

He closed his mind to the overwhelming yearning to do something that would shock her.

"What are you thinking, Giddy?"

"Nothing."

Her lips twisted. "I am thinking of nothing, too. I also think I have been very patient, and I'm ready for my real kiss now."

His breath caught. "Wouldn't you rather have a new rose bush for your greenhouse? I owe you a present."

"My birthday is not for another year now. I can wait for a present." She grinned. "But I want a kiss much sooner than that, tonight under the stars. From you. I won't forgive you if you try to trick me again."

She backed him against the tall tree she'd been hiding under before he realized she meant the kiss to happen right here, right now, whether he agreed to it or not.

Her eyes were fixed on his lip in the most disconcerting way. "Everyone said kissing is supposed to be painless and enjoyable," Jessica promised. "Don't frown like kissing me might be torture."

Dear God, it might be.

"Do you know how to kiss a woman so they enjoy it?"

Of course, he did. He wasn't a monk. "Yes," he admitted slowly.

"Show me?"

He glanced around, hoping for a reason to escape, but it was dark and there was no one on the estate grounds to distract her with at this time of night.

Kissing Jessica, no matter how chastely done, would change him...and how she saw him.

He was a trusted friend, but friends should not kiss unless—his heart raced—they intended to marry each other.

All the reasons he'd avoided entanglements with women seemed not to apply to the one standing before him now, however. Jessica demanded his attention, as always. But if she wanted to kiss someone for experience, his heart pleaded that he be the one to do it. He could restrain himself, and berate himself later.

He was very good at that by now.

He drew in a shaky breath before speaking. "Enjoyment depends on many factors."

Her smile was so bright, he almost staggered. "So you'll let me try? Thank you, Giddy! I swear you are the best friend I'll ever have."

He was the worst friend she had, if he could lose a simple argument with himself within the space of a minute. "It will only be once, and then we will never speak of it again. Not even to each other, and *especially* not to your father or your siblings."

"Of course not. My lips are sealed," Jessica promised—and then ground hers hard against Gideon's.

Gideon pushed her back then pressed his fingers to his bruised lips. "Ouch, Jess," he grumbled.

"Sorry, that was wrong, wasn't it?"

In so many ways that he couldn't say out loud. "A great deal too enthusiastic for a first kiss, I should think." He grabbed her arms to hold her back from throwing herself into a second attempt immediately. "Kissing should not be rushed. Let me show you how it is done. Slowly is best."

He bent his head and brushed his lips softly against hers.

Jessica remained still as a stone as he kissed

her again and again, little pecks upon her soft lips that were tender and sweet and everything she should experience the first time.

Unfortunately, his body clamored for immediate gratification and for him to continue. He yearned to hold her close against his body, no matter what the future might bring. Kissing Jessica was dangerous.

He drew back as soon as it seemed the right time, searching her expression for some indication of his success or failure.

Jessica had closed her eyes during the kiss and now licked her lips in the aftermath. "Hmm, you do that very well, Giddy."

"Thank you." He wiped his brow, glad a kiss hadn't changed anything between them. He was still *Giddy* to her, and that made him a good friend still, didn't it? The excitement was only on his side.

Her eyes opened suddenly. "Now it is my turn to kiss you."

Gideon groaned. He had counted on satisfying her curiosity, but he had entirely forgotten that this was Jessica Westfall he was kissing. She was the sort of female who liked to do everything in her own way and own time. He stood patiently in readiness for her next assault, hoping for a far gentler approach than her first attempt.

Jessica must have learned a lot from his kiss,

because all of a sudden she seemed much more sensual as she moved closer. His pulse began to race in response. She rested her hands lightly on his chest and looked up into his eyes. His heart hammered against his ribs as she slid her fingers upward until she could loop her arms around his neck.

She smiled up at him with all the trust of an innocent. "You are so good to allow me this little experiment. I was sure you'd be best."

"Make it quick, now."

Carefully, and with less force than the last time, she set her lips against Gideon's and kissed him the way he'd just shown her.

Their lips clung a moment as she drew back, and then she kissed him again—soft kisses that made him want more than anything to be younger, titled. A man who could trust himself to be what she needed.

Not the old family friend and neighbor everyone considered a bachelor for life.

He closed his eyes as she brushed against his body, drinking in the warmth that seeped through his clothing in a way that was far too arousing to be in anyone's best interests. He set his hands on her waist and told them to stay there, to hold her back from his body, no matter how things might progress.

Jessica's arms tightened around his neck, and she leaned fully against his hot body, sending a delicious thrill through him as his cock twitched against her belly. Dear God; as she kissed him with growing confidence, Gideon lost track of time and his reason.

He was suddenly cupping the back of her head to hold her fast to him, thoroughly committed to her education in pleasure. She made little sounds, soft whimpers, and a moan when their lips parted. Damn, but he was growing feverish for more of her, too.

He could imagine peeling her out of that scrap of a dress, baring her skin to his lips and eagerly satisfying every single demand she made for his attention.

His mind reeled with possibilities of a future together. Coming home to find Jessica waiting impatiently for him, making love to her under the stars or in his bed. Hot summer nights barely dressed, endless winters snuggled together for warmth and pleasure. A lifetime of Jessica in his arms.

And children—she would want children to hold.

He couldn't give her those.

He would not be a good father. He didn't know how.

Reluctantly, he eased his tight grip on Jessica and settled his palms back at her waist.

He opened his eyes as he pushed Jessica away from him firmly.

He would only disappoint her. He would not marry. Not her, not anyone.

He staggered away, breath churning from his lungs. He'd been weak to allow that kiss to go on for so long. Jessica deserved better from him than to be mauled.

"Gideon?"

He did not turn around. "Was that what you hoped for?"

"It was and more," Jessica said, and then she pressed her face against his shoulder. She leaned into him, silent for a change, but Gideon's mind was full of anger at himself. When Jessica wormed her way into his embrace and snaked an arm around his waist, he knew he had to break away from her soon. She must turn her attention elsewhere for future kisses. It was for her own good.

Gideon glanced down at the top of her head as the scent of her familiar perfume tickled his nose. Sometimes, when he'd spend a whole day at Stapleton, Gideon imagined he could smell her distinctive scent when he was home and alone again.

His heart raced again as she tipped her face up to his and searched his eyes.

"What are you thinking now, Jessica?"

"I'll tell you one day," she murmured before turning into his chest and hugging him.

It was nice to be held, and he reluctantly put

his arms on her smaller shoulders. The moment of passion had passed, and now they would be friends again. He let out a shuddering breath. Friendship was all a man with his history needed. "Brown will lock the doors of Stapleton Manor soon," he warned her after a few quiet minutes had passed.

"I have a key to the long gallery door, so I can sneak in and out whenever I please now."

Disturbed by that admission, he finally moved away from her. "Just how often have you snuck out on your own at night?"

"Just tonight. I swear, and only to see you. Never anyone else."

He was only mildly appeased by her statement. "You are not to leave Stapleton again on your own."

"Then how am I to see you without anyone knowing about it?"

"You shouldn't be sneaking off to see even me."

Her lips set in a stubborn line he knew well. "You can't stop me."

He took a menacing step forward, or at least tried to look intimidating. "I could warn your mother and have her take the key away."

"Oh, don't you dare," she complained. She pressed her hands over her bodice, which gave Gideon a clue as to where she was currently keeping the key. His pulse raced a little faster as the idea of retrieving it dawned on him. He clenched his jaw against the inclination. "Home. Now."

"Yes, Gideon," she said, all meek and compliant as she drew near once more. "I'll go straight away. As long as you promise to call on me, and no more making me wait days between visits."

He nodded slowly, knowing how stubborn she could be. He jerked his head toward the now dark manor house, though. "No side trips. Straight to your room and lock the door."

Jessica turned back to him, grinning. "Don't you trust me?"

He didn't trust himself. Not with her anymore. But there was also Lord James skulking about, too. "I know you all too well, my dear. Remain another moment and there's no telling the trouble you'll find yourself in with me," Gideon warned, nearing the end of his tether.

Jessica kissed him suddenly, and then danced back out of range of his reaching hands. "Good night, Mr. Whitfield. Pleasant dreams."

"Good night, Lady Jessica," he said, and then stalked behind her all the way home just to be sure she did go inside, waiting to be sure she did not come out again.

Chapter Twelve

---◆---

Jessica moved swiftly toward the front steps of Stapleton Manor where a two-wheeled one-horse gig was reported to be ready and waiting. When she had extracted a promise from Gideon to call on her today, she had completely forgotten about the race. So had he apparently. Of course he could not come now, so she would go to him.

She did not even need to take a chaperone for the short journey. The gig was built for one driver and one Tiger on the back. Plus, her father was already at Quigley Hill and expected her there shortly.

She tugged on her soft kid gloves and went outside full of great excitement for the day ahead.

Young Paulson, a young groom new to the estate, was standing at the mare's head, grinning madly. "Ready when you are, my lady."

"Thank you, Paulson."

She accepted assistance to climb into the carriage and arranged her skirts neatly around her legs. Once she had the reins and control of the horse, Paulson raced to the tiger's perch at the back and jumped aboard.

She clucked the reins once he gave the word he was settled, and the mare eagerly obeyed. Once beyond the turns nearest the house, she gave the horse its head. They sped off down the drive toward the stream crossing. The wind of their passage whipped across her cheeks, and she laughed out loud. She'd never have this much fun anywhere else.

Behind her, Paulson whooped with joy. "Are we racing too, today, my lady?"

"I don't wish to be late," she called back, never taking her eyes from the drive ahead.

When the gates to Stapleton came into view, and the creek crossing she slowed to a safer speed for the turn and then directed her horse toward Quigley Hill. The house itself was actually closer when walking. By road and carriage, she had a mile or more to travel.

As she neared Quigley Hill, she noticed the front lawns were dotted with many people from the village. It seemed the whole town had come out to watch the start. There were picnic blankets and chairs set beneath the shade cast by trees. There were even children running around, chasing each other.

She turned off the drive and slowed the gig to a stop, staying far enough away that her horse would not accidentally trample anyone or spook.

Paulson jumped down from his perch and ran forward. "Shall I help you down, my lady?"

She glanced at her timepiece and then the crowd ahead. There were a great many people around, and pushing her way through them all would take more time and effort than she might have before the start.

"No, thank you. I'll stay here for now, lad."

"As you like." Paulson rushed to the horse's head and took charge of the bridle, though.

Assured of her safety, Jessica tied off the reins. She shaded her eyes and looked around, wishing she'd thought to bring a parasol with her. Gideon was standing close to her father, Lord Rafferty, and Mr. Napier, laughing.

She nodded to Lord Rafferty and her father when they noticed her, but became distracted when Natalia suddenly appeared by her carriage.

"I thought you'd never get here," Natalia complained.

Jessica stretched out her hand to help Natalia squeeze onto the gig seat with her and looked back to where she'd last seen Gideon. "I would not miss this race for the world."

Natalia nudged her shoulder. "Doesn't Lord Rafferty have an air of danger about him today? He spoke to me, and I fairly shivered."

"He is always that intense."

Jessica frowned. She could clearly see Gideon but he'd still not turned to acknowledge her arrival. She needed him to know she was here to support him, too.

Natalia drew closer. "Can I ask you something?"

"Of course."

Natalia brought her lips close to Jessica's ear to whisper, "Is the duchess really increasing?"

"Yes," she whispered back.

"And she's not in good health?"

"Not always, unfortunately, but she's thrilled just the same."

Natalia giggled. "Mama was like that. She used to sing when she was increasing, even when casting up her accounts just before."

"Mama does not sing. Not yet, anyway."

Lord James strutted up to them. She took in his expensive silk waistcoat and gleaming riding boots and was not the least bit impressed. He presented himself as a wealthy man of good taste, instead of a heartless fortune hunter who had turned his back on a young woman who had probably loved him. "Good morning, Lady Jessica," he exclaimed.

"Lord James." She kept her response short, clipped. She did not wish to encourage him in the slightest. She had even waited until he'd ridden off that morning so she'd be spared the ordeal of talking with him again.

He eyed Natalia, and Jessica realized he'd forgotten Natalia's name or if they'd been introduced. They had been, too. A man like that didn't deserve to be reminded if he'd already forgotten someone so important to her.

A frown flickered in his eyes as she remained silent. "What a pretty pair you make in this quaint setting."

Jessica suppressed a groan when Natalia fluttered her fan and smiled shyly at Lord James. Natalia had always enjoyed flattery far more than Jessica. "Thank you, my lord," she murmured.

She looked toward Gideon again, and saw he was watching her at last. She waved, but he only nodded. He moved a few steps and bent down as a lady spoke to him. When they parted, Jessica saw Mrs. Beck.

Her breath caught as Gideon smiled at the woman.

Acid burned in her belly as he continued to talk as if he was in no hurry to leave Mrs. Beck's side.

He was called to his horse then and joined Lord Rafferty, who was already mounted and ready to ride. Mrs. Beck followed Gideon, too, while Jessica silently fumed. How dare he encourage that woman after their kiss last night?

Lord James cleared his throat. "Can I assist you down, my lady?"

She scowled. "What? Oh, I'm fine right where I am."

Her pulse grew loud as Mrs. Beck cast Gideon the most flirtatious smile Jessica had ever witnessed.

In public!

The harpy was practically drooling over *her* Giddy!

Her breath caught. "Oh, no," she whispered.

"Is something the matter, my lady? Do you need a refreshment or perhaps to sit in the shade?"

She glanced at Lord James, annoyed by his suggestion. She was no wilting wallflower who needed coddling, even if her heart had really begun to pound in her chest. "I am not in distress."

But she was in a way. She'd like nothing more than to scratch out Mrs. Beck's eyes right now for flirting with Gideon when *she* wanted to.

"Do not let me keep you, Lord James," she said as she waved her hand in his vague direction.

Lord James withdrew, but Jessica couldn't move a muscle, more for the shock and wonder filling her soul.

Natalia's hand stole onto her sleeve, distracting her from her stunning realization. "Lady Jessica," Natalia whispered. "Jess, you are staring…in a rather frightening manner, I must say."

Jessica blinked and looked down. "You were right," she whispered. "She means to have him."

"Do you mean Mrs. Beck? I am ever so sorry. I know you care for him," she whispered.

"I do," she whispered. Her chest tightened, and her breath came quick and shallow. "I love him," she admitted at last.

Dear God, I love Giddy so much. She darted a glance in his direction just as the race began.

He burst away, and she cried out. The crowd's wild cheers drowned out the sound. Within minutes, he and Lord Rafferty were just a spec of shadow disappearing around the first corner in the road.

Natalia hugged her quickly. "I know you love him."

"What?"

"I've always known," Natalia said with a half-hidden smirk on her face. "Took you long enough to admit it, but I don't mind that you didn't tell me sooner."

Jessica stared at her friend. "I...I didn't understand. Not until this moment. How could I not have known my own feelings for him ran so deep?"

Natalia hugged her against her side. "Love is like that, and I suppose it is not at all surprising, given the way he is around you."

"What do you mean?"

"He's always there, but makes light of your friendship. It is easy to miss his interest."

Jessica's heartbeat began to thunder in her ears. "Gideon is interested in me?"

"Oh, yes. It quickly became apparent to me once I spent a little time in your orbit. That the gentleman sees no other lady but you. He moves with you, though he tries to hide what he's doing. And you are always talking about him."

Jessica's face burst over with heat and shy pleasure. "I didn't realize."

Natalia shook her. "That is what makes you both an adorable couple. I don't know why he hasn't spoken up yet, but he should have long ago."

Because he never meant to marry anyone. Because of the way his own father had treated him as a boy.

Jessica closed her eyes. "What can I do?"

"Nothing until they come back," Natalia murmured, and then tugged on her arm.

"Come on. I'm desperately in need of a cup of punch if there is any left."

Jessica smiled quickly. "If there isn't, Cook will find something for us to drink anyway if we ask."

"I would be happy with water, honestly. It has become quite warm, hasn't it?"

She glanced at Natalia, and saw her friend was grinning madly. "Indeed," she agreed.

They clambered down unaided, leaving Paulson to stay behind with the gig, and strolled through the crowd arm in arm.

But Jessica's heart continued to beat wildly in her chest. She was in love with a man she'd never doubted would always be there when she needed him. Was it her turn to show him he didn't need to be alone after all?

A pleasant warmth filled her body at the idea of pursuing her own husband. Giddy had made a good show of pretending not to want to kiss her when he might have wished to do so very much. Oh, how she must have tortured him with her request for lessons. She would have to make it up to him.

Soon.

As they drew closer to a linen-covered table, a pair of chattering ladies cut across their path. Mrs. Napier turned, and then fell into step beside Jessica. "Isn't it a lovely day, Lady Jessica? My sister and I have been quite diverted by all the chatter. We are enthralled by Mr. Whitfield's beautiful grounds, too."

"Of course." Jessica changed direction when she saw the punch bowl was empty and the servants missing, but Mrs. Napier and her sister kept pace with them still.

"If you will indulge me. Lady Jessica Westfall, I must have the pleasure of introducing my dear sister, Mrs. Alice Beck, lately of Bath."

Jessica stopped walking and studied the other woman. She was pale, stiff-postured, arms held across her body as if she was extremely uncomfortable.

Jessica extended her hand, offering it to shake even though she had wanted nothing to do with the woman minutes ago.

After a brief hesitation, Mrs. Beck extended her right hand.

Jessica caught an expression of pain that flickered over Mrs. Beck's face before their palms connected. "How do you do?"

Mrs. Beck shook Jessica's hand lightly, and even so, she noticed the woman winced. "Very well, thank you."

Jessica released Mrs. Beck quickly and the widow hugged her arm to her body immediately. The woman was injured and trying not to show it.

Jessica glanced at Mrs. Napier, whose smile

revealed nothing—no concern, no guilt, either—but she had a tight grip on her sister's other arm. She returned her attention to Mrs. Beck. "I heard you have children."

"Yes, two boys."

"I simply adore children. Are they here today?"

Mrs. Beck shook her head. "Not today."

"They were left home, doing chores," Mrs. Napier cut in. "A little work is excellent exercise for idle minds."

Yet Mrs. Beck's expression suggested otherwise, and they were *her* children. Not Mrs. Napier's. Jessica did not like the way Mrs. Napier crowded her sister, either. She appeared to be almost a hostage.

"Well, I look forward to meeting them one day. Perhaps you and your sons could visit the duchess tomorrow at ten o'clock, Mrs. Beck. I understand from Mr. Whitfield that we have a common interest."

"I'm sure you'll be seeing more of my sister soon," Mrs. Napier said smugly. "Why, you never know, one day you could be very close neighbors indeed."

There was an obvious hint that Gideon was pursuing Mrs. Beck. Impossible for Jessica to miss or refute right now.

"I don't know about becoming neighbors," Mrs. Beck said quickly, a blush climbing her cheeks. "But I would like to meet the Duchess of Stapleton very much."

Jessica nodded. Once she got Mrs. Beck alone, she would discover the source of that injury and judge her intentions toward Gideon for herself. "We were just on our way to see what is keeping Mr. Whitfield's servants," Jessica muttered. "If you will excuse us."

She bid goodbye to Mrs. Napier and pulled Natalia away, her mind in a whirl. It seemed Mrs. Beck might not be the one pushing for a marriage with Whitfield after all. But Mrs. Beck did want something from Gideon, she was sure of that, too.

"Mrs. Napier is not happy you did not invite her to visit the duchess," Natalia warned in a quiet voice.

"I have my reasons for not wanting her there tomorrow." Mrs. Beck might be willing to speak freely without her tormentor, or tormentor's wife, silencing her.

Jessica knocked on the door to the servants' quarters and called out to Mrs. Harrow. From within, she heard the sound of rushing feet.

"Oh, is that you, Lady Jessica?"

"It is." Jessica hurried up the hall toward the kitchen. "Is anything amiss, Mrs. Mills?"

"It's Mrs. Harrow! She's taken a spell."

Jessica rushed inside to find Gideon's housekeeper slumped over the kitchen table.

She went to the woman and pressed her fingers to Mrs. Harrow's brow, noting the perspiration damping her hot skin, and then her wrist. "We should take her to her room."

Together, they half-carried the wilting housekeeper into her chambers and onto her narrow bed. The room was dim and cool, much better than the stifling kitchens, where the ovens were warming the air. "Mrs. Mills, you may leave her in my care. Please make sure Mr. Whitfield's guests have refreshments outside."

"You shouldn't trouble yourself over me, my lady," Mrs. Harrow insisted, trying to rise. "I'll be better in a moment."

"You've never been sick a day in your life, Mrs. Harrow," Jessica murmured, pressing a damp cloth to her brow that Natalia had thought to bring. "Just lie there and let me take care of you."

"Should we send for help?" Natalia asked as she fluttered a book about to create a breeze.

"No, not the doctor," Mrs. Harrow begged in fear, clutching at Jessica's hand.

"Shh," Jessica murmured, knowing many servants were terrified by men of medicine. "I think it is just the heat of the day, but it might be wise to have a second opinion."

"I was just too warm all of a sudden. I couldn't catch my breath."

She thought a moment, and then turned to

Natalia. "Could you find one of the older female servants from Stapleton and send them to me? There are a few here today. They will know what needs to be done for Mrs. Harrow."

From outside, the crowd cheered loudly and Jessica looked toward the window. "Is that the race ending already?"

"It might be," Natalia suggested. "Shall I go and see?"

Jessica glanced at her timepiece, noting only fifteen minutes seemed to have passed. "Please do. If Mr. Whitfield has returned, send him to me."

When Natalia was gone, Jessica touched the older lady's cheeks and then refreshed the cloth with cool water. She perched on the edge of the bed and smiled down at the housekeeper. "I think you're looking much better now, but you are not to move a muscle when Mr. Whitfield comes in."

Mrs. Harrow plucked at the blanket beneath her. "Never thought I'd live to see the day when a Westfall lady would tend a servant of Quigley Hill."

"It is no trouble," Jessica promised. "May I ask you a personal question, about the late Mrs. Whitfield?"

"The master's mother?"

Jessica nodded. "Was she ever frightened of her husband?"

Mrs. Harrow's gaze darted away but then she nodded. "She never complained."

"Did Gideon know what was going on?"

"Of course he did. Tried to stop his father, too, when he were young, only ended up getting more of the same. He was such a sweet little lad. His father tried to beat that goodness out of him." Mrs. Harrow suddenly caught her hand, eyes wide with fright. "You won't tell him I told you, will you?"

"Never, and thank you," Jessica murmured but her mind raced. Gideon had always been extremely protective of women, and now she knew why.

Jessica put her finger to her lips and made a shushing noise as heavy footsteps raced toward the room.

"What the devil is going on?" Gideon asked as he burst into the room, eyes a little wild as he stared at Mrs. Harrow.

"I am sorry, sir."

Jessica pressed the housekeeper back down when she tried to rise and turned toward Gideon. "Could we speak outside?"

He gulped and nodded, eyes a little wild still.

Jessica reminded Mrs. Harrow to rest and stepped outside, drawing the door closed behind them. "I think it is just a faint brought on by the heat of the day. I've sent Miss

Hawthorne to fetch a second opinion from an older Stapleton servant, though."

He raked a hand through his hair. "She's never sick."

"It happens." There were matters that affected women later in life, not that she could discuss them with Gideon. "I am confident one of the women I've sent for will offer the best advice for Mrs. Harrow."

He nodded. "Thank you."

She smiled up at him. "Are you happy?"

He looked up at her sharply. "Of course not."

"I meant about the race. You made excellent time today."

Gideon's expression changed to annoyance. "I did not best Lord Rafferty today. He forfeited the win."

She blinked. "How could he do that?"

"The man stopped in the shade to drink before we'd gone half a mile. He never intended to complete the usual course."

She laughed. "Perhaps Lord Rafferty wanted an excuse to refill your cellars with his wine?"

"It wasn't a fair race. I cannot accept the winnings."

She patted his sleeve. "You're always so concerned with doing what is right. It's one of the things I love about you, but I'm glad you're the acknowledged winner. Now you must escort me to the next ball."

"It isn't right to hold you to that wager," he said stubbornly.

She looked at him directly. "Do you not wish to claim the very first dance with me?"

"Yes, but…" His jaw clenched briefly.

The Stapleton housekeeper rushed up to her. "You sent for me, my lady?"

She turned away from Gideon and led the woman back to the housekeeper's room. "Yes, Mrs. Harrow is feeling poorly. Would you mind tending her for now and would you send for the doctor if you believe her condition warrants it?"

"Yes, my lady," she agreed.

As soon as the woman had gone into Mrs. Harrow's room, she returned to Gideon's side. "No buts."

His brow furrowed. "Our dance should be late in the evening. After you've had a chance to dance with the younger bachelors."

A shiver raced up her spine at his statement. He was denying himself, and she realized he'd always put himself last. "The first dance is yours, Gideon Whitfield, and if you don't claim it, I will not dance for the whole of the night."

He frowned. "But you love dancing."

"With you," she promised him, noting his brows rose in surprise. "I love dancing in your arms. You are my favorite partner and always will be. I always feel safe with you."

He shook his head. "You shouldn't."

She looked at Gideon, her heart pounding hard against her ribs. "I wish you wouldn't try to push me away."

He looked away suddenly, and her heart ached for him. "I need to tell you something before you hear it from someone else. I have changed my mind about Mrs. Beck."

Jessica rushed to cover his lips with her fingers. "Whatever you were about to say, don't do it." She stared into his eyes grimly. "I know you through and through, Gideon Whitfield. You are a good man. Kind, compassionate, and very gentle. You're willing to help anyone. But I saw Mrs. Beck today. She sees you as her savior from what I suspect is a terrible situation."

"What do you know about it?" he asked around her finger.

"Enough to intervene. I will speak to Mother tonight and Mrs. Beck will be helped, financially."

The air whooshed from Gideon's lungs. "Thank you."

"No man should ever marry a woman just to save her from pain someone else is causing her. That is not fair to you, when you deserve so much more." She dragged her finger from his lips slowly. "Promise me you won't ask her."

He sagged even more. "I promise."

"I will hold you to that," she warned. Relief that he would remain a bachelor made her smile again. "I know being my friend must be difficult for you. You must bite your tongue quite a lot so that you don't shock me. But you don't have to do that anymore. You can always confide in me too. I've always been full of questions, and I have a lot to learn still. You've always been there for me, and I want to do the same."

His expression grew stricken. "You don't understand."

Jessica touched his face. "Not until you share your secrets with me, too?"

To that, he seemed to have no response.

She smiled sadly. "I'm not a little girl anymore, Giddy. I'm not content with the crumbs of your attention. I want it all. I trust you completely. I have since I was a child."

He nodded slowly, and then shook his head. "I do care about you, Jessica."

The passion in his kiss wasn't pretend. But to have more, he'd have to want it, too. "I know."

He looked away.

She waited but she couldn't force him to reveal that he might love her. He'd had a long time to become this way. If they were to have any future together, he'd have to admit that he wanted more for his life. She waited a little longer then sighed. "I had better go before anyone comes looking for me."

Jessica stepped around him and walked away with a heavy heart.

Chapter Thirteen

———— ♦ ————

Gideon pushed his hair from his eyes and settled his hat back on his head, but his heart was pounding so hard against his ribs he was almost breathless. As much as he hated disappointing Jessica, he had no choice. She was never meant for someone like him. The kiss had been a terrible mistake he couldn't take back.

He followed her outside to the party, knowing there was nothing he could say that would make her understand. They were never meant to be more than neighbors, friends, no matter the astonishing passion that had flared hot between them, catching him completely by surprise. He had overwhelmed her last night, that was all, and she had been swept away by the romance of their midnight rendezvous.

Jessica thankfully did not look back. Her back was stiff as she spoke to her father, then moved on to talk to her friend Miss Hawthorne for a little while. Eventually, she disappeared into the crowd, and he hoped she was enjoying the sunny day and not thinking of him.

He tried not to look for her again. He shouldn't, but the habits of a lifetime were hard to resist, and when he wanted to find her, to no avail, he grew concerned. He moved through the crowd, restless and uneasy about how they'd parted. She would never understand the terror he felt when he imagined any future with him as a parent.

"Oh, there you are, Whitfield."

Gideon could groan, but he schooled his features and smiled as Lord James bore down on him. "My lord."

"Congratulations on your fine win."

He sighed but kept his real feelings about the matter to himself. "Lord Rafferty gave me an excellent start."

"Excellent form for a gentleman of your years," Lord James exclaimed.

Gideon took offense at that. "Rafferty and I are almost the same age."

Lord James colored as Gideon glared at him. "Any chance you might have a moment for a word?"

Gideon looked about them but hadn't a clue what Lord James could possibly want. Gideon had been trying to avoid him today. The man's waistcoat made his eyes water.

Gideon nodded slowly. "I have time now."

"It is a private matter."

Stranger and stranger. He gestured toward the side gardens where only a few people lingered. "What can I do for you?"

"I am in need of assistance."

"With what?"

"Lord Stapleton's daughter. I want her."

Gideon nearly staggered at the way he spoke of Jessica. "I beg your pardon?"

"Well, you're…" Lord James gestured up and down. "You are uniquely placed to ensure my success and bring your influence to bear. You've known the family a long time, being neighbors and all."

Far too long to like the direction this conversation was headed. "Indeed."

"It's clear to see Stapleton trusts your opinion. The man talks about your easy good nature all the time."

"Does he?"

"The thing is…I have botched my affairs quite thoroughly, and I need your help to win her hand in marriage."

Learning to notice when a lady isn't interested in you might be a good idea, Gideon almost said aloud. "I've never been married, so I wouldn't know how to advise you about a courtship."

The fellow frowned deeply, lips tightening

until the skin around his mouth puckered. James squinted at him. "How much?"

"I beg your pardon?"

"How much for your estate?"

Gideon grew cold all over. "Quigley Hill is not for sale."

"My father says everything is for sale." He leaned close. "If I dangle my purchase of such a prime estate before Stapleton, one conveniently close, he'll see the merit in the marriage. Agree to sell Quigley Hill to me now, and I'll make you a rich man by the end of the month."

"I'm rich enough. More than you, I've heard."

"Marriage will restore my coffers and overflow yours." Lord James' face became set. Hard. "But you are not titled. I can make that happen."

He stared at the man in shock. "You're offering me a title?"

"My father can arrange anything."

Gideon's chest expanded with fury. Jessica's affections could not be bought, not with *his* help. He took a menacing step toward Lord James, fists clenched. "Get off my land before I kick you to the boundary, you impudent whelp."

Lord James narrowed his eyes. "You're making a mistake," he muttered, but spun on his heel and stalked away.

A heavy hand landed on Gideon's shoulder and squeezed. "Come back, little lordling, and let Whitfield kick your pampered arse,"

Rafferty called out softly, mocking Lord James. "Grasping bastard, isn't he? Father is much the same. I'd have punched him in the nose."

"Tempting."

Rafferty got in front of Gideon and set his fingers to his chest. "Was it my imagination, or are you unsurprised by his plans to wed Lady Jessica?"

Gideon pushed his hand away. "I knew about the possibility a few days ago."

"Stapleton really does like you, to share that juicy tidbit," Rafferty mused, rubbing his chin. "I've always found the family rather standoffish."

"A few of them are."

Rafferty started to chuckle. "The pretty one has you well tangled up in her affairs."

Gideon scowled at Rafferty rather than answer him.

"Well, she won't stand still for that sort of treatment." Rafferty smiled quickly. "Stubborn. Set in her ways already."

Gideon shook his head. "You're describing Mrs. Warner, not Lady Jessica. For all that they are sisters, Mrs. Warner is not as easy to manage as Jessica has been."

"Women are never easy, and they always want to manage *us*." Rafferty grunted. "So, do you intend to propose to her?"

"Who?"

Rafferty rolled his eyes. "Lady Jessica."

Gideon did not answer that.

"Wait too long, and you'll lose your chance." Rafferty chuckled evilly. "Or are you afraid you'll disgrace all men on your wedding night when you fail to get a rise at your advanced age?"

Gideon glared at Rafferty. "Not likely."

"Not with her beauty in your bed, I'd wager." Rafferty looked at him slyly. "Why haven't you gone after her yet?"

Gideon pinched the bridge of his nose. "Rafferty, do be quiet. I'm about ready to throttle you."

"I'd pay to see that. I've never known you to lose your temper in all the years we've been acquainted." Rafferty lifted his fists though, throwing a few harmless punches into the empty air between them. "Despite your advanced age, you've still got some fight left in you, I'm sure."

"We're the same age," Gideon ground out.

"I'm younger." Rafferty chuckled. "What's the problem?"

Rafferty had no idea about his childhood, the beatings he'd endured so his mother would remain unharmed. "Too much."

Rafferty dropped his fists, looped an arm about Gideon's shoulders and shook him. "Have you never once been in love?"

Gideon almost felt sick to his stomach, especially when thinking of Lord James and

Jessica alone together.

Rafferty seemed not to need his answer and kept talking, walking with him back into the crowds. "Tell me, what would you do to win Lady Jessica's hand in marriage?"

Anything.

Gideon tripped over his own feet but Rafferty held him up. "Steady on, sir, or should I fetch your walking cane or a sedan chair, perhaps."

"Would you shut up and let me think," Gideon grumbled.

He'd overcome any obstacle to be the right man to keep her safe. He brushed his hand over his mouth, realizing that for all his hesitation, he might not be able to live in peace without Jessica in his life. He wasn't sure if that was love or his need to be the one to make her happy. He could have had her last night, but his protective nature got the better of him.

Love? Perhaps, but he'd no idea how to prove it. None at all.

"Thinking. That's definitely your problem," Rafferty warned. "Trust me, I've been through this before. You just have to throw yourself into the chase and hope to come out on top. You need any pointers for the courtship?"

"No."

When he spotted Lord James skulking about, cozying up to Jessica's father, he scowled. Lord James had the advantage of proximity. "Maybe."

"I'm your man, and I have the perfect solution to your courtship woes. Come with me."

Gideon followed Rafferty all the way to the Duke of Stapleton's broad back, a little worried by Rafferty's enthusiasm to see him leg-shackled at last.

"Whitfield has just given me the perfect idea, your grace," Rafferty called out.

The duke turned, a frown marring his face. "Oh?"

"It is well past time you invited us both to stay, like the old days. Wine, and a song or two until dawn. What do you say?"

"Dear God, I was hoping you'd forgotten how to sing. But," Stapleton's face grew still, and his eyes darted to where Lord James stood a little to the left, "if Whitfield stays, too, then I can't see the harm. We'll make it a proper house party. A week or two, but no sleeping on the dining room table this time, Rafferty. My daughters are old enough to make an example of you."

Rafferty and Stapleton discussed particulars of their invasion of Stapleton manor within the hour.

Gideon's head spun at how quickly his future might be changing from what he'd always expected. The dispatch of servants to bring fresh clothing for them both was underway, and to soften the impact of their stay, Gideon pledged his winnings, the wine Rafferty had wagered, to Stapleton's cellar instead of his own.

Tonight, he would sleep under the same roof as Jessica and had no impetus to return to his own home for the next two weeks. A man might win a woman's hand in marriage in that space of time...but could Gideon win Jessica's understanding, too?

When he looked at Lord James again, smiling as if the party were for his benefit, he vowed to protect Jessica forever.

Stapleton clapped him on the shoulder suddenly. "You are a true friend to save my family from another night of tedium. I swear that pair talks of nothing but their own ambitions day and night."

"I'm glad to be of service," he murmured, then winced.

Pursuing Jessica for his wife could put his friendship with the Duke of Stapleton in a whole new light. He'd have a father again.

———— ◆ ————

Jessica slunk back to Stapleton, dejected by Gideon's rejection of happiness. She gave her horse an absentminded pat, slipped a coin to Paulson, and climbed the stairs to Stapleton

Manor's front door very slowly. Why couldn't Gideon see that she was grown enough to be...his?

The knowledge that he didn't want her the way she thought of him made her both angry and miserable. For a year, she'd endured talk about the qualities she should look for in a potential husband. Gideon embodied every good and kind attribute a spouse could, and his name had never been mentioned. He'd even participated in several discussions. Admittedly, his remarks had been supportive of not rushing any decision, which she'd attributed to him being a bachelor of long standing.

Stapleton's butler opened the door for her and welcomed her home, and she answered him with just a nod. Maybe Gideon didn't want her after all, or perhaps he didn't want a wife of any description.

She'd taken three steps inside the cool interior, hadn't even removed her bonnet and gloves, before Rebecca was suddenly upon her. She blinked at Rebecca stupidly, tears beginning to prick her eyes.

"I need to talk to you in private," Rebecca said as she grabbed Jessica's hand and towed her toward the music room. Jessica stumbled as the door was thrown shut behind them with remarkable force.

She turned around quickly. "What?"

Rebecca stalked toward her, apparently very angry. "Who. Is. He?" she ground out, eyes blazing.

Jessica took a pace back from her sister's unexpected fury. "Who?"

Rebecca grabbed her arm before she could retreat farther, holding her tightly until it pinched. "You were seen last night, meeting with a man."

Jessica was not a good liar but she had to try. "I wanted some air."

Rebecca leaned close and ground out, "And the man you left behind? You will tell me his name this instant."

Jessica swallowed hard. "It's not what you think."

It was probably worse.

"Who were you with?" Rebecca was so angry her mouth was pinched white around the edges. Her grip tightened even more as the silence lengthened. Rebecca could cause a great deal of trouble for Gideon if she wanted to. "Were you meeting with Lord Rafferty?"

"No!" she cried. "I was with Gideon."

Rebecca released her immediately and turned away. When Rebecca began to pace, arms folded across her breasts, Jessica's heart started to pound in time with her hard steps.

"What are you going to do?"

Rebecca paused and then turned, smiling

with triumph brightening her eyes. "Nothing. For now."

Jessica was afraid of that smile but stood her ground. "What do you mean, 'nothing for now'? What about the gossip you heard?"

"Gossip is unavoidable on an estate of this importance."

"But—"

"No buts. We will do nothing and allow the rumor to spread."

Jessica paled. "Father will be angry at me. At Gideon, too."

"You should have thought of that before you started flirting with Father's best friend." Rebecca wagged a finger.

Jessica gaped but then snapped her mouth shut. She had been drawn to Gideon more since her return home, but she hadn't quite considered what she'd been doing as flirting. Not really. But if she loved him, her behavior was completely normal. She looked across at her sister and winced. "I'm sorry if my actions have disappointed you."

"I knew something was in the wind at dinner last night, but the duchess swore Whitfield was merely being protective. Possessive is more likely." Rebecca came close and put an arm around Jessica's back. "What you start must be finished."

It took her a moment to work out what

Rebecca might mean. "You mean you *want* me to marry Giddy?"

"I wanted you to marry a duke's son but, as always, my little sister has had everyone wrapped around her finger since her first breaths," Rebecca stated with a touch of bitterness Jessica had noticed before but never dared point out.

"It isn't my fault the family doted on me," Jessica protested. "I would gladly trade places. Everyone had such high hopes for me that it's suffocating."

"Better than being overlooked altogether," Rebecca whispered, almost to herself. She looked up quickly, eyes softening. "You can do no wrong in Father's eyes, and he will, of course, forgive you for any indiscretion in the end. I assume the duchess is unaware you've been encouraging our neighbor?"

"She doesn't know about last night." Jessica moistened her lips. "What do you think? About Giddy and me?"

Rebecca sighed and then, lips pursed, neatened Jessica's hair, pushing strands behind her ears before she spoke. "I've nothing to say against him."

"But he's older. Twice my age, in fact. Some people might consider that strange."

Rebecca shrugged. "My husband was older than me, too, so I do not consider it a disadvantage. Marrying an older man can have many benefits, in fact."

Jessica couldn't contain her relief at the news. She'd imagined Rebecca would hate the idea of Gideon as her husband. Rebecca had always pushed Jessica toward younger men, especially ones with a title. She caught Rebecca's hand and squeezed her fingers tightly. "What are they, the advantages?"

"Generally, older men are sensible, long since leaving their wild days behind; frugal, and we both know Whitfield is sensible and is as wealthy as he could possibly be. He can afford a wife, even without your dowry, though he should be encouraged to employ more servants once you are wed."

"Giddy is not always sensible," she said, defending him. "He let me kiss him."

"Sensible in the way he conducts himself in society. I highly doubt him capable of causing a scandal that might embarrass the family at his age." Rebecca smiled slyly. "And now that I know you have kissed, I'm even more determined that you should marry him. Eventually."

"Eventually?"

Jessica sank to the music stool, and Rebecca joined her at the instrument. Rebecca laid her fingers on the keys softly and played a sad tune. She had once been the musician of the family.

Jessica had longed to play half as well when she'd been a girl and had always admired her sister's skill on the instrument.

Everyone said Jessica had surpassed Rebecca at a young age, and she was always first to be asked to play, now she thought about it. Rebecca's bitterness was understandable she supposed, but still not her doing. She folded her hands in her lap, content to listen to someone with more experience.

After a moment, Rebecca glanced sideways at Jessica but continued to play the sad tune. "Older men do not rush when it comes to marriage. It is one of the challenges you must prepare for. If Whitfield proves resistant, however, I shall have no hesitation to exert a little pressure to bring him to the point."

"I won't have you threatening him," she warned.

Rebecca shrugged. "I highly doubt I will need to say a word if you continue to persuade him to kiss you back. He'll do the right thing in the end."

Jessica's heart began to pound. "That does not sound hopeful."

"Well, you've chosen a worthy adversary." Rebecca let her hands settle on the keys. "Gideon has certainly had his share of admirers. He's proved quite adept at avoiding entanglements over the years, even the most blatant ones."

Jessica's eyes narrowed. "From whom?"

Rebecca frowned. "Jealousy is an unbecoming emotion in a lady, little sister. You must learn to curb your possessive tendencies when you marry Whitfield. You will meet many people who have a history of friendship with him that you cannot share and may never fully understand. You must always remind yourself that he married *you*. That must be enough."

Jessica bit her lip. Gideon had lived another life while she'd been in the nursery playing with her dolls. She had to make a place for herself beside him somehow. "He doesn't want things to change."

"Men never do. They like to believe the decisions they make are always their own." Rebecca smiled. "He will learn soon enough that Lady Jessica Westfall will always have her way."

Jessica gripped her sister's arm and hugged her fiercely, grateful that Rebecca approved of the man she loved. "Mrs. Rebecca Warner can have hers, too."

Rebecca stood suddenly. "Mrs. Warner is far too old for daydreams and late for an appointment. I advise you not to waste any time capturing Mr. Whitfield's complete attention."

Chapter Fourteen

———— ✦ ————

Gideon stepped from the shadows and halted Jessica's flight into the gardens. "I thought I told you not to come outside alone again."

Jessica rushed to him, flung herself against him and hugged him tightly. "I was hoping to see you alone before I went to bed. I'm so glad you're here. I want to apologize for earlier. I always expect you to have the answers, but clearly you haven't."

"I'm sorry, too. I do care for you, more than I ever expected I could." He quickly took a step back, determined to do what he'd intended. Starting a courtship with a woman you've known since she was months old was complicated, and he wanted to do this right. "You've seen me now, so please go back to your room. You'll see me tomorrow. His grace invited Rafferty and I to stay a week or two, you know. I'll be here until your unwanted suitor is long gone."

"I am not going to go back to my room." Jessica laughed softly. "Come along, Giddy. I'm going to see the stars from the top of your hill tonight. Nothing will stop me."

She moved off without him. Save restraining her, which wasn't a very gentlemanly thing to do, he really had no power to stop her exploring the grounds unchaperoned in the dead of night. He'd made a vow when she was a child to protect her, and another earlier today, and a gentleman never went back on his word. He couldn't allow her to come to harm, so he would follow at a distance.

Jessica gave a little devilish laugh—and then suddenly sprinted off into the trees.

Minx! She hadn't tried to elude him in years. He shook his head and gave chase, rushing through the woods with no care for himself. Having her disappear and reappear ahead of him was maddening, and he caught up to her as quickly as he could.

He grabbed her hand just before they reached the top of the hill and stopped her mad flight. He spun her about in a circle. Jessica shrieked but then fell against him, appearing happy to be caught.

Her hands slid up his chest in a sensual caress that wasn't in any way proper. "You are still faster than I am, sir."

"Years of chasing after you have kept me fit." He warned her, "Do not run off again."

"I won't."

She sounded contrite, but he was reasonably sure she was enjoying herself immensely as she clung to him. No doubt about it, she'd planned this escape. She'd been counting on him to follow her.

"Come and view the heavens with me." She strolled away a bit, and when she went to sit on the grassy slope, he quickly offered his coat for her to rest upon.

Jessica removed his spectacles from the pocket before they could be broken and perched them on top of her head. Gideon snatched them back and held them to keep his hands occupied. "What are we doing here, Jessica?"

"Being together," she murmured, settling to the ground. "I could never see the stars in London."

She stretched her hand toward him, fingers beckoning as she did the other day, and then folded her arms behind her head and lay down on her back. Gideon closed his eyes, but the vision in white silk and lace was burned into his brain. She remained silent, obviously finding nothing wrong with her request.

He opened his eyes as he moved toward her. He sat a safe distance away—if there ever was such a thing around her now.

She turned to face him, and he swore her eyes were laughing at him. "I don't bite."

Gideon might. He dropped his gaze to her breasts, nearly spilling from the bodice of the elegant gown she wore tonight. This was almost torture. His traitorous prick thickened at the notion of feasting on her body. He swore under his breath and lifted one knee to hide his unfortunate condition from her.

"We sat closer than this at supper," she protested.

"There were chaperones. You can hear and see me well enough from over here." He frowned. "Tell me what you want from me, Jessica."

"I would have thought that obvious by now."

"Say it."

"Very well. I want *you*, Mr. Whitfield."

His head spun for several minutes. Quite a definitive answer. Not one he could misinterpret. "Well, all right then."

She placed one hand on the ground and leaned toward him. "Do you fear for your virtue around me now?"

He shook his head, fighting the pull of attraction toward her. If she knew the manner of thoughts her words put in his head, Jessica might fear for her virtue, too. "Not exactly."

"It is nice, isn't it, being so far away from everyone? We can speak our minds and not worry about being overheard." She rolled onto her side, using her hand to support her head, and looked right at him. "I never imagined you would blush, but you are, aren't you?"

He gave her a stern look. "You should be blushing, too, young lady. Running off alone with me in the middle of the night again. Your family would be scandalized."

"Fanny wouldn't be. She'd love me no matter the scandal I caused."

"Mrs. Warner would never let you forget this if she found out," he warned her. Mrs. Warner might shoot him first and force a marriage while he bled out at her feet.

She laughed then and rolled onto her back. "Lie down next to me, Giddy. No one else will know about tonight unless you say something."

She had no idea the thoughts she put in his head with her innocent remark. He couldn't control Jessica, but he longed to put her in her place. Beneath him would do, and since she seemed to want that, too…

And then he had a very hard time erasing that image from his head.

Despite the temptation, Gideon moved a bit closer. "I'll know."

"Did I tell you I've had *the talk* seven times? From different people. I swear my family and friends are more obsessed with my love life than they should be."

He blinked. That was quite a lot. No wonder she seemed different. Bolder than ever. "Seven times?"

"Mother, Rebecca, Fanny, and even Mrs. Hawthorne and Natalia have had their say, although Natalia hardly speaks from experience. My last governess spouted a lot of nonsense mother said should be ignored."

"You said there were seven. Who else?"

"Samuel."

"Dear God, I hate to think what advice your wayward brother might give to you."

She smiled quickly. "He said that only I would know who I wanted, and that I shouldn't be bashful about saying so when I had decided. He said the gentleman would appreciate a woman who didn't play games."

Well, that explained a lot about the changes he'd noticed in Jessica. She was certainly more direct in telling him what she wanted. "I'm not sure whether to thank Samuel or strangle him."

"I've been thinking of the gift I gave you for your birthday, too. Samuel was astonished that I was so particular about what I had made, so perhaps I've been thinking about what you need longer than I ever realized."

He glanced her way. "What do you imagine I need?"

"Hmm." Shivers raced over his skin at the sound. "Oh, look, a shooting star!"

"Where?"

When she pointed, he leaned closer to share her view, but there wasn't another following the first.

After a moment of waiting without another sighting, he realized she'd just tricked him into moving closer. "There was no star, was there?"

Jessica chuckled. "Only the one tonight."

When he inhaled, his lungs filled with the sweet, familiar scent Jessica always wore—lavender from his own garden. He looked her way reluctantly, only to be disconcerted that she was looking right back at him—and she was very close.

Moonlight illuminated her face, making her seem ethereal and delicate and utterly spellbinding. An angel. He had known this woman as a child, but he was having a difficult time remembering the little girl in the face of her bright beauty.

Her fingers rose to touch the tip of his chin, and she lightly brushed against the grain of his night beard. "I like that you want to protect my reputation, Gideon, but I don't ever need protection from you."

"Yes, you do," he confessed, rolling away from her, onto his back.

She laughed. "Would you kiss me again, please?"

He concentrated on the stars wheeling in the heavens above them as he considered her request. Not a good idea given the early state of their courtship. They shouldn't even be together now. "We should go to bed."

Jessica spluttered.

"I didn't mean together," he rushed to promise. "I meant to our *own* beds. Separately. You on your side of the manor, me on mine."

"I'm not going to bed till I've had my kiss for today, and I don't mean the kind you gave me the first time." Jessica rolled onto her stomach and crawled closer. "Kiss me like you did last night, just to be sure I remembered everything you've taught me."

Gideon couldn't breathe as she crawled even closer and positioned herself nearly on top of him. Her knees where both at his side but he could easily imagine pulling her down until she straddled him. Gideon was trapped by his own lustful thoughts and felt his control of the situation slipping from his grasp yet again. He could barely think beyond the yearning to fulfill her request to kiss her.

Her fingers moved to his cheek, and then her fingers threaded into his hair at his temple. She was becoming very seductive in the way she touched him, and against his better judgment, if he'd ever had any, he lifted his head. He pressed his lips to hers in a tender kiss, intending it to be as short as the last one.

Their kiss lasted a little longer than all their kisses combined, and he tried to slide away from the pressure of her body against his. "There."

"Goodness," she whispered, flopping onto his chest, pinning him down and rested her chin on the back of her own hand. "Your kisses just get better and better, don't they?"

"If you say so."

"Indeed I do say. Can we kiss again?"

He wrapped his hands about her upper arms, intending to push her off him if necessary. She had no idea what she was saying or how her words tortured him. "Why? Wasn't that enough to satisfy your curiosity?"

"Not nearly enough." Her expression grew serious. "Who knows when you might grant me another."

Gideon let out a tortured groan and looked past her head and up to the heavens. "Why me?"

She patted his chest. "Should I have let Lord James catch me instead?"

He looked into her face quickly. "Not if you'd like him to remain alive."

"You don't approve of him?"

"He's not the man for you."

"I agree." Jessica snuggled a little closer. "He's not you."

"I am going to regret this one day," he warned.

"But not tonight," she promised. "Tonight, I want you to be proud of me."

His expression softened. "I've always been proud of you, Jess."

"This is different."

"It is."

She looked away briefly. "Natalia says that a man might stick his tongue in my mouth while kissing me. Is it horrible?"

He lay still beneath her, and worried about all those *talks* she'd endured. Too much information or wrong information must be confusing. He lifted his hand to Jessica's head and gently turned her face to his. "Not when done right."

"Show me," she begged, and slowly lowered her lips to his.

Their kiss began as the others had, but with Jessica hovering above him, tension quickly built between them. After due consideration, Gideon gently rolled her onto her side. He rose above her, his intention being to control their kisses. He gently cupped her face, slid his fingers along her jaw, to her throat, and behind her shoulder.

Jessica did nothing to stop him touching her body whatsoever. She eagerly embraced what they were doing together, and that worried him. Her arms wound around his neck and slowly pulled him down toward her.

Remembering her new request, he rolled her to her back, keeping his body at an angle to hers, and then ran his tongue along the seam of her lips. Jessica gasped.

Gideon took advantage of her surprise and teased his tongue into her mouth.

Jessica inhaled sharply, and he felt her wriggle in response. He had to place the heel of his hand firmly on the apple of her shoulder to prevent her from rolling into him. Things could quickly get out of control between them if he did not exert his will at least a little. This was supposed to be a slow courtship after all, but Jessica was much too eager. She clearly thought she could wrap him around her dainty fingers. He was not so far gone as to not see the risks of giving her what she wanted when she wanted it.

A soft whimper escaped her when he pulled back. "That is enough," he said, gasping slightly.

Jessica collapsed back to the ground, gasping as well. "I think so, too."

At least she could be sensible. Kissing led to bedding, and it was much too soon for that. He might need time to undo some of the poor advice she's been given by well-meaning family and friends.

He burst to his feet, taking a few steps away as he pretended to brush himself off while discreetly adjusting his arousal. Kissing Jessica was exciting but it was far too soon to reveal the lust she stirred in him. "Get up, and we'll sneak back inside."

"Thank you, Giddy," she whispered. After a moment, she stood, lifting his coat from the ground. She shook it out then lifted the garment to her chest. She hugged it a few moments and then held it out to him.

Gideon quickly donned the coat and, after a moment, decided he might just pass inspection in the shadowed hallways of Stapleton Manor so long as he did not linger. He found his glasses in the grass, amazed they'd avoided being broken as they'd rolled around, and slipped them into his coat pocket again. "Let's go."

She rushed to his side and linked her arm with his. "How did I do?"

"As always, you are a quick study," Gideon promised as they began the long walk back to the manor at a slower pace. Gideon would have a lot to become used to in the coming weeks. "You won't see me until late tomorrow."

"Why?"

"Your father wishes for a gentleman's morning, shooting and such."

"Then I will see you for luncheon," she insisted. "I'll expect you to sit by me. We're having mushroom soup."

His heart lightened at their little joke on the world. Mushrooms *were* a boring subject. Hardly anyone knew about them, which meant they could say whatever they liked—utter nonsense mostly—and no one ever challenged their exaggerations. "Lord James is not fond of eating them."

"Such a shame, and that is why I insisted a mushroom course be added to every meal during his stay. We're using some of the spices I found in London tomorrow, too. I'll need your opinion on whether you'd like to eat any of them again. I want to tell Mrs. Harrow your reaction."

"I see." He put his fingers to her face, lightly touching the softness of her jaw. "That is kind of you."

"I like your servants," she whispered—and then froze. "Someone is standing ahead of us."

He pushed Jessica behind him and moved them into the shadow of a wall. They pressed close together, hoping not to be noticed. When the figure eventually withdrew to the house, Gideon could breathe easy again. "That was too close for comfort."

It was only then he discovered Jessica had wrapped her arms around his waist and had buried her face in his cravat. She seemed quite adept at cuddling up to him, he'd noticed. He brought his hand up her arm and slipped it behind her head. Her face rose to his, and she kissed him one last time.

Fast courtship or slow, he had a feeling being proper around Jessica wasn't going to be easy.

He jerked back. Their near miss might become a real scandal if he forgot himself. "No more moonlight meetings," he whispered. "Please."

"But—"

He cupped her face in his palm. "I'll find you tomorrow, I promise."

"Good." Her lips found his again, and then she was gone, darting back toward the house with nary a sound to give her away.

Chapter Fifteen

———— ♦ ————

"Can someone dim that infernal racket?" Lord Rafferty complained, holding his head as he squinted across Gideon's fields.

Gideon handed over the flask of brandy. "Medicine."

Rafferty took one look, and then snatched up the flask and took a deep swallow. He wiped his mouth with the back of his hand. "Whose idea was this?"

"Yours." He held his gun over his arm, barrel pointed down at the ground. Shots rang out ahead of them. Stapleton and Lord James were making one last sweep of the area before calling it a day.

They'd had unfortunate luck on Stapleton's estate, so they had moved to Gideon's property at his suggestion.

Gideon was biding his time now, waiting

until all guns had been fired and the servants had taken them and their game back to the manor before he broached the need for a private conversation with Stapleton.

"A friend would not have pointed that out." Rafferty pinched the bridge of his nose and then squinted up at the sky. "Are you really going to talk to him today?"

"Yes, or else he'll find out the worst way that his daughter is running around the estate at night."

"With you."

"With me." He jerked his head up as Stapleton handed off his gun to the estate manager. "Remember your promise to distract Newfield and the son."

"The things I do in the name of friendship." Rafferty stood and came to his side. "Did you hear him as we crossed the brook? He's such a poor opinion of women that even I was offended. Keep them at home, their minds fixed on running a household, and advised me to never leave a serious news sheet like *The Times* lying about for my daughter to read."

Gideon gritted his teeth. "Makes me wonder if his first wife expired of excessive boredom."

"I had the same thought. Newfield is careful to hide his opinions around the women, though. Lord James does, too. I wonder what

Mrs. Warner would do to Newfield if she knew what he'd said of her sex."

"Tempting, but let us not have the summer end with a murder."

"It's been years since Becca truly had a good reason to get worked up over a man," Rafferty chuckled evilly.

Gideon glanced at Rafferty in surprise at his use of a family nickname for Mrs. Warner. Hardly anyone did that anymore. "I don't believe she's entirely forgiven you for the last time you goaded her into a confrontation. What did she call you?"

"A degenerate drunkard with no sense of decency."

"You did climb into the wrong bed in that house party, completely drunk—and naked—and refuse to wake up until morning."

"The host gave her a softer bed than mine," Rafferty complained.

"I'll owe you for this if it turns out well." He took a deep breath as Stapleton reached them at last. "All done?"

"Yes, I think that should be sufficient," Stapleton said.

"Yes, yes. Quite a productive outing. You must reconsider my offer," Lord James suggested.

"What offer?" Stapleton asked.

Rafferty already knew from eavesdropping,

but still asked, "Yes, what offer?"

Gideon shook his head, but Lord James was only too happy to explain. "Made him a generous offer for the property. I still think I can persuade him to part with the place. What do you say, Stapleton?"

"I'd say he's a fool to consider an offer under a hundred thousand pounds, which is what *I* would offer him if I ever thought he might consider a sale."

Gideon choked. So did Lord James. It was a ridiculously high amount to suggest for his small slice of the county. "I said no. Quigley Hill is not for sale."

Stapleton clapped a hand on his shoulder and didn't let go. He cocked his head at Rafferty. "You lot go on. We'll catch up with you shortly. I need to have a word with my neighbor."

Rafferty nodded and encouraged Lord Newfield to walk ahead with him. Lord James frowned, but followed his father across the field.

Stapleton waited until they were gone before speaking. "If you needed money, you should have come to me first."

"I have more money than I know what to do with. I did not start that conversation, nor ever would," Gideon insisted. "I am never leaving my home just because the man thinks to buy his way into a marriage. He wants to buy Quigley Hill, but intends to pay me from Jessica's dowry and no doubt his father's pocket."

Stapleton narrowed his eyes. "You realize they came to take Jessica from us?"

Gideon nodded.

"Neither man has spoken to me directly on the subject, but the marquess is dropping hints left and right. I do wish Lord James would just spit it out instead of stringing it along. I'm never giving my daughter to such a lapdog."

Gideon sagged with relief. Jessica would not be wed to a fortune hunter. She was free, and so was he to do as his heart desired. "So you'd prefer Jessica's suitors to get straight to the point."

"Gods, yes. I've married off two daughters already. I know who's worth encouraging and who isn't."

Gideon glanced at his feet briefly then back up. Now or never. "I'd like your permission to court your daughter."

"Yes, that is exactly what I wish Lord James had done in the first place."

Gideon frowned. "Stapleton. Your grace. I am asking for *myself*. I have grown fond of Jessica and would like your permission to court her."

The duke's brow furrowed. "You cannot mean that?"

"I am deadly serious."

Stapleton looked around them. "This is a joke, surely. A means to amuse me."

"I would not make the request as lightly as that. I am serious. I would like to marry Jessica, if she will have me."

The duke stared at him a full minute, in which time Gideon gave thanks that no guns were within easy reach. The duke turned away and walked off a short distance, not toward Stapleton, however. He was walking deeper into Quigley Hill.

Gideon watched him go, assuming he needed time to gather his thoughts. He would return soon, so Gideon waited nervously for his response.

He did not wait long. The duke rushed toward him, bristling with indignation. "Let me understand you. You ask today if you can court my youngest daughter. A girl you have known her whole life."

"Yes."

"When you waved her goodbye in January, did you know you would offer for her after her season?"

"No. I had no intention of doing so."

"No intention of doing so then." The duke advanced another step. "But you did think about her in that fashion, without the intention of offering for her."

He shook his head. "I always believed Jessica

would end the season a married woman. I thought I would not see her again before that day came."

"So as soon as she returned, unmarried or betrothed, you...what? Suddenly decided you were done being a bachelor and had to have her?" The duke poked him in the chest. "I trusted you!"

"I never overstepped my bounds while she was not out."

"But afterward, after the expense of her presentation and an unsuccessful season, you have?"

"I kissed her, and so it is only right that I act like a gentleman and make my interest known to her father."

"Where did you kiss her?"

"In the garden."

The duke balled his hands into fists. "And what did my daughter do to make you think you had the right to kiss her?"

"Jessica did nothing wrong."

"Forgive me if I do not agree. Jessica never caused me trouble before you came along."

Gideon gritted his teeth. "I have been here all along, soothing her childish tantrums, explaining matters she didn't understand when you were too busy to give her your time. I took away the bottle you intended to drown yourself in when your wife died," he added for good measure. "She'd never been kissed before."

The duke snorted and shook his head. "So of course, she accepted her lessons from good old Uncle Giddy without a word of complaint."

Gideon clenched his hands at his sides now. Nothing Stapleton said was anything Gideon hadn't already thought about himself in the past day. "You make it sound like I forced myself on her! I certainly did nothing to harm her."

If Stapleton knew the truth, that it was Gideon who was pursued for kisses, he might be more understanding. The duke adored his youngest and would not like to hear that truth.

Stapleton blinked, drawing back. "I apologize. I didn't mean to imply that you were like him."

Gideon controlled his temper. Being compared to his father was the highest insult. Stapleton had known his father, *and* the brutish nature he'd hidden behind closed doors from almost everyone. "Accepted."

Stapleton shook his head. "No. You may not court my daughter."

When he gave no further explanation, Gideon reeled back a step, even though he'd expected that answer on some level. He was without a title, without a great fortune to his name.

He swallowed the lump in his throat. "Well, then. Thank you for hearing me out."

"We'll just forget the matter," Stapleton announced.

"Of course." He bowed his head to hide his dismay and gestured for Stapleton to leave.

The duke, however, stood his ground. "You *are* coming for luncheon, aren't you?"

Gideon looked up slowly. "I did not imagine you would still want me there."

The duke scowled. "Don't be so dramatic. As you said, it was only a kiss. Easily forgotten, and already forgiven."

Not so easy to forget for Gideon.

And now the real torture would begin—invited to visit her home but not allowed to pursue the object of his affection. Stapleton couldn't have picked a better punishment if he'd chosen one deliberately.

Reluctantly, he fell into step with the duke, and they soon caught up with Lord Rafferty, Lord Newberry, and Lord James. Rafferty tried to catch his eye, but Gideon looked away each time. He didn't want to see the pity he might find in Rafferty's eyes.

On the grounds of Stapleton's great estate, he spied Jessica returning to the house. She glanced his way several times but didn't change her direction. He was glad she stayed away. He'd no idea what to say to her after his talk with her father.

The duke decided to continue on his walk,

away from the manor. Gideon declined to join them, so did Rafferty, claiming fatigue. Gideon's heart was too heavy right now. He didn't know what to do.

The only good thing to come out of today was the knowledge that when Lord James did eventually ask for Jessica's hand in marriage, he'd be turned down.

Gideon headed inside to the boot room and left his muddy boots to be taken care of by one of Stapleton Manors many servants. Then he dashed up the nearest staircase and into the guest bedroom he'd been assigned to for the duration of his stay.

He closed the door and swore softly under his breath, certain this was going to be the hardest day of his life. Now that he'd finally spoken of his interest, he didn't look forward to the future. A future alone, a bachelor for life, seemed an unsettling idea now.

When he glanced across the room, he spied a sealed letter on his pillow. He reached for it, noting there was nothing written on the outside to give away the contents or who might be sending him missives here.

When he pried off the blue wax seal, Jessica's elegant penmanship on the papers jumped out at him. He folded it quickly and pushed it under the pillow without reading a word.

He flopped back on the bed and put an arm

over his eyes. He should have known Stapleton wouldn't let his daughter marry just anyone who dared ask. The duke was much too protective. Slow to change, also. It had taken Stapleton a good long while to marry a second time.

Gideon sat up slowly, eyes wide. Stapleton might just need time to become used to the idea that he was interested in Jessica. He'd said no to a formal courtship, but that did not mean he could not assure Jessica that he was genuinely interested in marrying her.

Stapleton had been difficult over Fanny's late husband, too. He'd made Lord Rivers, a wealthy peer, jump through a great many unnecessary hoops before finally giving his blessing to the marriage. Lord Rivers had never complained—and Rivers had never given up, either.

Gideon nodded. He would do well to follow that example.

———◆———

Jessica paced the long gallery, fretting that Gideon might not see her letter in time.

But as the long gallery door emitted a soft groan, she realized she should have had more faith. Gideon slipped into the room. When he shut it just as quietly, her pulse began to race.

"Giddy."

She moved toward him, a little uncertain, truth be told. Last night, she'd been with him, enjoyed his kisses so much that she'd been thinking of him all day. The way he'd touched her; she wanted more of that. But she wasn't certain he did too.

He grinned as he came closer. "How was your morning?"

"Quite productive. Mother agrees the village girls could benefit from having instruction. Mrs. Beck will move into my cottage with her boys tomorrow. Lessons will begin as soon as she is settled in. I even managed to find a position for that farmhand's sister. Twice a week, Miss Sweet will clean and do laundry for the new school and Mrs. Beck."

He grinned. "You did all that in one morning."

"Not just me alone." She closed the distance between them and laid her hands on his chest. "Having Mrs. Beck restart the old school was originally your idea. I offered up my cottage and Mama approved the funding. Papa had already agreed to that last night."

"We make a good team, don't we?" He smiled, warming her all. "The note you left on my bed could have gotten you in trouble. Why did you want to see me? Was it just to tell me what you've done for Mrs. Beck?"

"No." She swallowed. "I just couldn't wait to be alone with you again."

When he cupped her cheek in his palm Jessica leaned into the touch.

"Don't risk your reputation over me. I'll always be here for you. No matter what."

Relief filled her. "Good."

Gideon lowered his head the remaining distance and at last kissed Jessica the way she had been dreaming about all day. Jessica wound her arms around his neck and pressed herself against him tightly. Gideon did not hold back his passion today. He held her close, and allowed the kiss to continue until she was growing hot and very bothered.

Jessica pushed at him, forcing him against a wall. She brought her hands up to tangle in his hair, loving that she could touch him, and that he seemed to like her doing so.

He wet his lips. "We have to stop."

"Why?"

"Luncheon will be announced soon. We are expected to sit down with everyone shortly."

She pouted and caressed his ear. "I don't want to go. I like this."

"I do too, but I will not have your reputation called into question."

She understood his concern, even if she didn't like it. "It's not fair."

"No, it is not. Patience."

She tried not to smile. He would be just down the hall tonight. If he would not meet her in the garden, the other option was to visit his room. "Patience, and then we might do other things together tonight."

He kissed her lips. "We have to slow down, but no matter what you hear, remember, I'm not going anywhere."

"Neither am I." She met his gaze again. "Giddy, who do you imagine my husband might be?"

"I never liked to speculate before." He pressed his lips to her brow and peppered kisses over her skin. He drew back too soon. "I hope he will be the man who already loves you very much," he whispered.

A nervous laugh escaped her, and she wound her arms tightly around his neck. She hugged him, and he responded by lifting her feet from the floor and twirling her about in a circle.

"I can tell that pleases you but," he set her back down to earth to look into her eyes, "I fear your father will begin to talk of taking you back to London to continue your season soon."

"Why?"

He traced her jaw with his fingers and she shivered all over. "So you might meet more eligible men."

"Oh? What? No!" There was no one more

eligible to be her husband than *her* Gideon.

"Jess," he said carefully. "I am much older than you."

"That's obvious."

He sighed and released her. "In case you haven't noticed, I don't have a title, either, which has long been a requirement of your father's."

She set her hands to her hips. "I don't care about that."

"But your father does, and you could, too. I would hate for you to become bitter like Mrs. Warner one day, reminding everyone every moment of every day that she's a duke's daughter. She married beneath her, even if her husband had funds enough to make him acceptable."

Jessica shook her head. "That is not actually why she is bitter. It's my fault, sort of. She hates that I'm the favorite." Jessica stared at him as her words sank in. "You are handsome and kind, you make me laugh. You are someone I could grow old with."

His brow crinkled. "I'm already old."

Jessica loved to shock Gideon. She grasped the lapels of his coat urgently. "Then we should waste no more time. We should elope."

Gideon's eyes widened in shock, and he stumbled away from her. "Absolutely not!"

"Why not?"

Gideon paced away a few steps and then turned. "Because if we eloped, your new mother could not attend your wedding and your father might never speak to either of us again."

"Oh." The appeal of an elopement died instantly. "Having my parents at our wedding was something I was looking forward to."

"Never suggest eloping again," he warned.

"Yes, Giddy," she murmured in a tone she hoped conveyed agreement. However, she would not rule out returning to the subject at a later time.

"Do not be concerned, I'm not in my dotage yet," he promised, and his grin was decidedly wicked.

"No, you are not." She grinned at him. He seemed very lively when she was in his arms. "Now, where were we?"

He frowned at that. "What do you mean?"

She sauntered forward, adding a little sway to her hips. "I'm old enough to know what I want, and that, my dear sir, is more of you."

Gideon backed up a step. "We should discuss a plan for the next few days."

Jessica smiled in triumph as he collided with another wall. "We'll manage to see each other without anyone suspecting, the way we did at Christmas."

She placed both hands on the wall either side of Gideon's shoulders, preventing his escape. He tugged at the cravat around his neck as if he were too warm. "We'll be on our best behavior until Lord Newfield and Lord James leave. If only we could send Mrs. Warner away, too."

"Oh, Rebecca will not be a problem. She might even be a help," she suggested. Jessica pulled his head down and kissed him until it was time to join everyone for luncheon.

Chapter Sixteen

With the issue of her future husband decided upon, Jessica smiled much too much. Her sister suggested she moderate her expression so that Lord James was not encouraged by mistake. Her mother smiled indulgently, and Father asked if she was feeling at all well.

Gideon merely watched from afar, his cravat slightly askew from her earlier handling of him and a knowing smile hovering on his very kissable lips.

Being married to him would be lovely. The more time they spent alone together, the more Jessica's imagination and hopes soared for the future. She'd had the talk from seven people after all, so she knew what to expect and, combined with her new experiences kissing Gideon, she nearly couldn't sit still.

She ached where she perhaps ought not to.

She had the most incredible urge to cross the room and perch herself on Gideon's lap. She hadn't done that since, well…it must be years now. Although she was sure that, once on Gideon's lap, she would behave in a different manner than she ever had as a child.

"The proposal must become law. Reform cannot wait," Lord Newfield insisted, banging his fist on the arm of his chair.

Ugh, politics again. Would Lord Newfield never be quiet? Gideon had been willing to read to them tonight, but he'd never had a chance to do more than suggest a book of poetry.

Father shook his head. "No. No. In its present form, the bill will never pass."

Lord Newfield glowered. "Progress will not be halted by a dozen men determined to keep their monopoly in the north intact."

Father grew still, and Jessica's smile slipped. Father opposed the current bill before parliament, but not because he had any pecuniary interest. The proposal was obviously flawed and unfair.

Tension mounted as Father and Lord Newfield engaged in a staring contest.

"Lady Jessica, might I prevail upon you to play the pianoforte again this evening?" Gideon asked suddenly.

"Yes, a fine idea," Rebecca agreed, her eyes widened—encouraging urgent agreement with

Gideon's suggestion.

"Of course, but only if you will play with me tonight," she suggested to her sister.

"Yes," Gideon agreed. "We can all take a turn tonight."

"Oh, no," Rebecca and Mother each cried out in protest, causing Jessica to laugh.

Gideon shrugged. "I'm not *that* bad."

"Would you excuse us?" Jessica went to Gideon, hooked her arm through his and drew him toward the music room. "I hate to be the bearer of bad news, Giddy, but you are simply awful on the pianoforte."

"Misjudged unfairly," he cried as Father and Lord Newfield resumed their argument. Mother and Rebecca trailed behind, each offering the other a chance to play with Jessica first.

Jessica looked over her shoulder as Father and Lord Newfield's voices rose louder than ever. Poor Papa. There were times when his life seemed unfairly boring.

Lord James followed, silently, thank heavens. At least he could withhold his opinions on occasion. She turned away from him without smiling.

A set of maple drawers contained all the music the family owned, and Gideon opened the drawer containing duets. "So many to choose from," he said as he began to shuffle through the collection.

Jessica winced. Giddy really was terrible. For a man who had a lovely instrument sitting idle at home, she couldn't account for his lack of skill. His mother had played beautifully until the day she died, she'd heard.

He chose one sheet at last, turned for the instrument and sat down at the bench before Lord James could beat him to the spot.

Jessica exchanged a resigned glance with Mother and then sat at his side. She read the music sheet he'd placed before her, noticing it was a very old one she hadn't played in years.

Lord James, denied a chance to sit beside her, hovered near the instrument—obviously keen to take Gideon's place the moment he rose. Jessica took her time reacquainting herself with her part, and then braced herself as she glanced at Giddy. He had to start first. "I'm ready."

"Good." He fitted his eyeglasses and raised his hands to the keys.

And then he played. Perfectly.

Jessica gaped in shock and continued to stare as he performed his part of the piece flawlessly without her. He glanced her way, one eyebrow raised. "This is a duet," he noted. "Shall we try again?"

"Yes." She gaped still. Mind reeling. Gideon knew how to play the pianoforte. "Yes, please."

She faced the keys and played with him, the

first time she'd ever enjoyed doing so. They played to the end, and then his fingers left the keys. The silence was startling in the wake of their performance. "Whenever did you learn to do that?"

"I took lessons as a child. My father did not approve and made me stop, but while you were gone to London, I found an instructor to refresh my memory," he confessed, a slight smile turning up his lips. "Not so terrible now."

"No indeed. But as you've always told me, practice will help. There is nothing you cannot do once you set your mind to it."

"I wanted to surprise you when you came back," he touched the tip of her chin with his knuckle, "you've no right to tease me about how terribly I play now."

Astonished and so very pleased, Jessica hugged him quickly. He'd done it for her, she was sure. From now on, she wouldn't play duets with any gentleman but him. Especially not Lord James. "Thank you, Giddy," she whispered. "We'll be able to play together all the time soon."

He laughed softly as he reached for the music sheet and folded it closed. "Anyone would think I did something unusual."

"Not unusual for you, but very agreeable." Excited, she jumped to her feet. "Shall I find another we can play together?"

He shook his head and stood up. "Let us hear you with Mrs. Warner next."

"But—"

He leaned close. "It took me all the months you were away to perfect that one."

"I'll teach you another, starting tomorrow," she decided, grinning at him shyly.

Gideon smiled back too. "I was hoping you wouldn't mind helping me along with my lessons when you have the time to devote to my instruction."

She shivered at the suddenly husky tone of his voice. Later, when they were married, when she was his wife, her life would be devoted to him in so many ways.

She turned away as her pulse kicked up speed. The problem with suddenly feeling desire was that she'd not the faintest idea what to do with herself while the sensation lasted.

"When might you have the time to spare *me* a moment of your attention, Lady Jessica?" Lord James cut in bluntly.

Jessica looked up at Lord James, noticing his suspicious stare and clenched jaw.

She moved toward Gideon. "Never, my lord."

Gideon put his arm around her shoulder briefly. "Jessica mentioned you spent a great deal of time with Lady Hannah Alexander during the season. I'm familiar with the family.

I went to school with her uncle George for a time. Fine family. Not a hint of scandal anywhere in the ranks."

Jessica caught Lord James' eye. "Lady Hannah must be missing you as much as I did Mr. Whitfield while I was in London. She did seem quite taken with you."

Lord James' eyes narrowed on them. "Yes, Lady Hannah is a fine woman. Very proper," he murmured with a frown for their proximity.

That was almost an accusation that Jessica was not! Undeterred, she smiled anyway. She would be married to Gideon. Soon, she expected. "We hope to read happy news about you both soon in the papers."

Lord James took a pace back, but his eyes flickered to Gideon, questioning. "I hope to read a similar notice for you, too."

"There will be," Gideon promised.

Lord James ran a hand over his mouth then scratched his head. "Would you excuse me? I need to be…somewhere else, I think."

"Of course," Gideon said as he held his hand out to Lord James. "I wish you good hunting."

"Groveling is always a good idea," Jessica suggested as the pair shook hands. "But hurry. You never know who might be trying to take your place in her heart."

Lord James nodded and then rushed across

242 | HEATHER BOYD

the room. The young man said good night to Mother and Rebecca, who had remained locked in their own conversation.

She and Gideon stood side by side for a moment, and then he turned to her. "I *really* missed you, Jess."

She grinned. "You did?"

"Every damn day you were gone was agony," he admitted with a shy shrug. "I tried not to worry, but I'm not very good at that."

"What did you worry about?"

"That someone else might love you as much as I wanted to," he admitted.

Jessica laughed. "Then I am grateful my season was such a failure."

He drew close. "It wasn't a failure. You came back to me."

She nodded but she could feel tears forming in her eyes.

She turned away before he noticed, but Rebecca was watching them now, a triumphant smile hovering about her lips.

Jessica ignored the smile and moved toward her mother. "What were you pair talking about?"

"Christmas."

Jessica let out a sigh of relief. At least Rebecca hadn't revealed her pursuit of Gideon to Mother yet. She wanted to be the one to tell her.

"Mrs. Warner has offered to organize everything for Christmas this year," Mother murmured with a smile of gratitude. "And I have agreed."

Jessica smiled. "But—"

Mother placed her hand on her expanding middle. "I will be a new mother at Christmas, and I don't know how difficult this little one might be."

"She will need to rest. Before and after," Rebecca murmured, eyeing the small bulge with a frown of her own.

Jessica stared at her sister, wondering what she really thought about the impending addition to the family. Rebecca had never had children, but she was very good with their brother's children. Everything they both knew about birthing a child came from observing other women go through the experience. But it was kind of Rebecca to offer her help with the manor. "Are you going to stay in the country then? Stay at Stapleton until the child comes and beyond?"

"If Father will allow it," she murmured. "I'd be happy to."

"I'll convince him." Mother's statement shocked Jessica so much, she gaped.

Neither one of them had liked the way Rebecca had behaved toward Gillian last Christmas. When Jessica had not been paying

244 | HEATHER BOYD

attention, Mother and Rebecca seemed to have made peace, and that was such a relief, too. When she married Giddy and moved to Quigley Hill, Rebecca would be here to take Jessica's place.

She looked up as Father entered the room. Thankfully, he was alone. "Well. That went as well as expected."

Gideon turned away and poured Father a whiskey. "What did you say?"

"What I needed to." His expression grew sour as he looked at Gideon. "A word, if you please."

"Of course."

The pair moved aside and spoke privately for a few moments, Gideon's back growing stiff with every word spoken, while Father became more expressive with his hands.

The pair turned, Father revealing annoyance, Gideon's expression unreadable.

The pair took chairs on opposite sides of the room, Father at Mother's side, Gideon alone. Both offered up false smiles when Jessica caught their eye.

"Jessica?" Rebecca called. "I have found the perfect music for us."

Troubled by the tension she sensed in the room now, Jessica hurried to her sister's side and looked at the sheet she held out. It was a complicated piece of music to play, one that gave her the most trouble. "Are they arguing?" she whispered.

"I suspect so. Father has been watching you both all night, and he is clearly not happy with what he sees," Rebecca warned. "What progress have you made with directing Whitfield to the outcome we discussed?"

"The best outcome imaginable. He admitted he loves me."

Rebecca exhaled. "Thank heavens. Now we can work on Father. I am sure Newfield brought up your future tonight and was refused. Can you hear the servants rushing about above us?"

Jessica concentrated and heard more noise than expected at this time of night. "Oh I hope Lord Newfield and Lord James never come back."

"Let us hope so. But no matter if they return. We'll have the time we need to convince Father to let you marry."

"Let me?"

Rebecca smiled wryly. "You may have gone to London to find a husband, but father has never believed anyone would be good enough for his daughters. We still have a battle on our hands to make him accept your loss."

Although she meant to have Gideon for a husband, she did not really want Father unhappy about it. Gideon was a good man, kind, thoughtful and her friend. Her father's friend, too. They were neighbors, and she couldn't stand the idea that loving her put them at odds.

When they sat down to play, the tension in the room eased a little. By the end, when Mother announced fatigue, Father left the room with her.

Jessica put her hands in her lap and looked across at Gideon, feeling stricken with uncertainty. He smiled, but it never reached his eyes.

He rose to his feet slowly and came closer. He complimented them on their performance and then drew in a large breath. "I am afraid I have been recalled home and must beg your forgiveness for my leaving."

"What has happened?"

"Nothing you need to worry yourself over."

"Father has sent you away," Rebecca said quietly.

Gideon nodded. "I must go."

Jessica exchanged a glance with Rebecca. "When will you be back?"

His smile slipped. "I am not certain. My possessions are being packed as we speak. You will have to make do with Lord Rafferty's poor company, if he ever shows his face."

Jessica burst to her feet. "I will see you out."

"I am not sure that is a good idea," he advised. "It is not proper."

"Rebecca?"

"Patience," Rebecca cautioned.

She merely stared at Gideon, overwhelmed with disappointment that he had to go. "Oh, to hell with that," Jessica muttered under her breath. She'd let Gideon leave and follow him later.

Chapter Seventeen

———— ✦ ————

Gideon sighed as the door beside him eased open and Jessica, clad now in a darker gown, appeared beside him on the terrace outside the long gallery. She startled when he made a soft sound to announce his presence but grabbed his outstretched hand quickly. Gideon closed and locked the Stapleton door securely, tucked the key into his pocket, and led Jessica into the empty, dark garden, keeping to the shadows. They said not a word to each other until they were on Quigley Hill land.

"I thought I was clear about not doing this," he complained.

"But I needed to see you," she promised. "I want to know what's going on."

"There is nothing to worry about. I told you I wouldn't give up," Gideon promised as he took her in his arms, smiling down at her fondly. "No matter what your father does or says, I'm in love with you. I will wait forever for him to accept that. What did you want to say to me that couldn't wait until tomorrow or the next day?"

"What are we going to do?"

"There is nothing to do. Lord James has already gone. He called for his horse as soon as he left us, and he's no doubt headed directly for Lady Hannah's door to beg her forgiveness for abandonment." He pressed his head against Jessica's and inhaled the scent of her hair. "I wonder when your father will realize you've gone."

"He won't," Jessica promised, running her hands up and down his chest. "I made sure everyone saw me go to my own room and into bed."

He stilled her hands before he became too distracted. "He is your father, and he knows you as well as I do. If I can anticipate your every move, so will he."

"Let's hope he doesn't." She looped her arms about Gideon's shoulders. "Did you ask Father's permission to court me?"

"It seemed the right thing to do. A certain young lady was not content with finger kisses."

"The ones from your lips are better."

"Wait till I've kissed you all over, then you'll really be impressed." He laughed softly but heard her breath catch at his suggestion. "Kisses can be anywhere, Jessica. Lips, neck...elbows."

"Elbows?"

He grinned slowly. "I didn't want to shock you by naming the *real* place I was thinking about kissing you."

"Where is that?"

"I'll leave you to imagine. We've been alone too long as it is."

"I'm not going home yet," she said stubbornly. "Take me with you so we can continue talking."

Although he should not, he eased closer. "You know what will happen if I take you home with me. We will probably not talk at all."

"What is wrong with that? I want *my* suitor to tell me more about passion tonight."

"That would be the study of a lifetime, not one single night in my bed."

She toyed with the buttons on his waistcoat. "You'll give me that lifetime soon enough."

"I will," he promised, looking forward to those blissful days ahead.

"Then we start tonight, and tomorrow, and the next day and the next."

He shook his head at her. "There really is no stopping you now, is there?"

"When I gave you my heart, you got the rest of me, too."

Jessica's hands spread on his chest, and then

she gripped the lapels of his coat. "I need you, more than I've ever needed anyone in my life."

His pulse raced at that admission. He might need her just as much, too. "Just how much were you told about intimacy?"

"I blushed quite a bit," she admitted. Jessica took his hand and placed it on her breast. "And now my skin heats whenever you are near."

He moved his hand until his thumb brushed over her nipple. Jessica gasped but did not pull away. "Hmm, I begin to suspect your instruction was a bit more explicit than strictly necessary."

Jessica laughed and hugged him. "At least I know enough not to be afraid. I actually look forward to certain aspects; being naked with you is one."

He drew her closer. Jessica continually surprised him with her willingness to explore the desire growing between them. It made him a little crazed, imagining all the things he could do to her in his bed with her permission. He lowered his head a little more and pressed his lips to the skin of her neck. A ragged sigh left her lips, and she turned her head to give him better access.

"I want to be with you," she whispered.

He debated refusing her, but being alone with her was what he wanted, too. "All right."

He scooped her up into his arms and began walking.

Her arms tightened about his neck. "Where are we going?"

"My bed."

Jessica cuddled against him and fell silent as Gideon carried her home. His house was dark, his servants long since gone to bed, he suspected. They encountered no one as they went inside.

Gideon was a little puffed by the time he reached his bedchamber, though he tried not to show any fatigue. He eased Jessica down onto her own feet so he could shut and lock the door quietly behind them.

While he shrugged off his coat, Jessica drifted away, moving through his room, studying his possessions in the poor light. He caught her expression when she passed the window—she was smiling as she looked at everything that mattered to him. She stopped near the bed, where the robe she'd had made for him rested. She turned around and leaned against the foot of his bed. "Well?"

He drew near, looking for signs of doubt. He should have known better though. She had chosen—him.

Jessica lifted her hands to his cravat as soon as he was close enough and concentrated on untying the knot.

Gideon let her attempt it, and then finished the job when she proved unequal to the task.

He pulled the long length from his neck and stood to wait for what Jessica would do next.

She unbuttoned him from his waistcoat and started on his shirt sleeves. "I've never wanted to undress a man before."

"I'm happy to hear that." Gideon lifted a hand to her hair. "How many pins should I look for?"

"A dozen."

He searched for them, pulling them out gently. His breath caught when Jessica's dark hair hung loosely about her shoulders. He'd expected it to be longer. "Did you have your hair trimmed?"

"While I was away." She touched her head self-consciously. "It's not too short, is it?"

He ran his fingers through the soft, silky strands. "I was only surprised, not disappointed that you'd cut it."

"It's lighter, easier to pin up now."

"You always look lovely."

She tugged his shirt up without bothering to unbutton his breeches, and Gideon reached over his shoulder to pull the garment over his head. Jessica splayed her fingers over his bare chest before he'd even managed to toss it aside.

"Oh my," she whispered. "Your skin is so warm."

Her hands on his body were torture but sweet. She poked him, squeezed his biceps and made him feel more manly than he'd ever felt before. He turned away to sit and remove his footwear, taking his time in case Jessica decided to leave.

Instead, she removed her slippers and set them neatly under the bed, as if his bed was already hers.

When he stood again, she came forward, and her fingers went to the waistband of his breeches. He sucked in a breath as she figured out how to unbutton those, innocently brushing her fingertips against his erection. When his breeches began to slip from his hips, he caught Jessica against him and made a meal of her willing mouth.

He kicked off his breeches and left them on the floor.

But knowing he couldn't avoid his unveiling much longer, he eased back a little and waited for Jessica's reaction to his nakedness.

A smile played over her lips as she gazed at him, then she brushed her hand along his length. Her touch made him close his eyes, fighting a shudder of want that coursed through his soul. She explored him eagerly, thoroughly, as she did everything else he'd ever introduced her to.

She found moisture at the tip of his erection and teased her finger over the head.

"Hell," he grumbled, and then clenched his

jaw to stop further outcries. They had to be quiet, or they would be found by his servants— women who must always respect Jessica.

Jessica chuckled softly. "Men really are as sensitive as Fanny claimed."

He looked down at her and shook his head. He would strangle Fanny the next time they met. "Especially there."

She nodded and maneuvered him to sit on the edge of the bed. Gideon got a glimpse of their future love life then and there. Nothing surprised her—and nothing would stop her being with him. Jessica was having an excellent time seducing him. He wasn't at all unhappy about that. He *was* going to marry her.

He eased back on the bed at her urging.

"Take off your clothes," he whispered.

She grinned. "I thought you'd never ask."

Her fingers flew down the line of buttons at the front of her gown, and when she shrugged out of the garment, she was bare beneath.

She'd come to Gideon, traipsed across two estates with him, wearing nothing but a thin gown!

He reached for her and dragged her naked onto the bed with him. They kissed and kissed, until they were both panting and feverish with lust. Gideon explored her curves eagerly. Pressing kisses as he moved down her body.

Jessica sighed and panted to each caress, her

fingers tangled in his hair. When he reached her breasts and made love to them, her moans and enthusiasm for what he was doing left no doubt that she was enjoying herself.

He ran his fingertips down the outside of her long legs, and then detoured toward her soft inner thighs. Jessica breaths began to churn, and he looked up at her quickly. She said nothing...not even when he moved his fingers to the apex of her thighs. She trembled a little and bit her bottom lip to muffle her moan. Gideon moved to a more comfortable position, so his face was directly over her sex.

"That's where you wanted to kiss me, wasn't it?" she asked in a rough whisper.

He nodded. "This is where I *will* kiss you, repeatedly, as often as you want me to."

She collapsed onto her back and widened her legs for him. Intrigued, he teased his fingers through her hair and then parted her gently. Jessica twitched a little as his fingers explored her folds. He found her already damp, and the scent of her arousal nearly undid him.

Keeping a tight grip on his desires, he found her clitoris and played with her. Jessica threw an arm over her eyes, her other over her mouth, and even so, her moans took on a desperate edge.

He lowered his head and kissed her once, twice, a third time. And then he flicked his tongue across her as she cried out in surprise. He settled in to feast on her hungrily.

Jessica grabbed his hair suddenly, holding him against her sex as if he wasn't close enough. He sucked a little, licked a lot, and it wasn't long before Jessica was writhing—lost in passion.

Gideon pushed her thighs wider with his shoulders then pinned her body in place. He loved her until she bucked and thrashed against his face and gasped his name.

He eased her back to earth with soft kisses, and then moved up her body slowly, taking his time before meeting her eyes again.

She had a dazed look about her, and she'd never looked more lovely with her dark hair spread across his pillows. He braced himself above her, keeping his weight on his arms as she came back to him.

She wet her lips. "Oh my. That was…"

He grinned and aligned his hips with hers. "Only the beginning."

Jessica shifted beneath him, glancing down to where his hips pressed against hers. "I can still feel the sensations."

He nodded. "That's the way it should be."

He was in no hurry to bed her, but he eased his hips into position. He raised one of her legs and set her foot on the mattress beside his hip. Jessica lifted the other on her own.

She touched his face, caressed his cheek, smiling the whole time. "I'm ready."

Gideon set his hand over her hip and tilted her up a little. "I know."

He pressed forward with steady pressure, stopping when Jessica hissed and braced herself against him. She remained that way a while, and then softened slowly. When she was relaxed enough, he pushed in farther, but this time her fingers only stroked him.

When he was inside her all the way, he lowered himself to his forearms. "You are amazing."

She smiled as he began to move. Her fingers tangled in his hair once more, and she closed her eyes. "This is lovely," she whispered after a while. Her eyes opened slowly and locked on his. "I can feel you inside me. You're exciting me again."

Gideon groaned and buried his face in the crook of her neck. He moved his weight to one arm and pushed his fingers between them to tease her sex once more.

Jessica ground against them eagerly, and he let her drive their passion even higher.

"Stay with me. Don't... Please," Jessica begged as her back arched once more, and her body thrashed in the grip of a second release.

Gideon lost what was left of his control and muffled his groan against her skin. Panting hard, body hot and slick, he attempted to roll to his back so as not to crush Jessica while he caught his breath.

He might have succeeded if she'd released him.

As it was, Jessica followed him, draping herself loosely over his body, gasping for breath too.

He settled a hand behind her head, holding her against his chest as their mutual passion faded to a lovely memory.

After a moment, Jessica stirred. "Fanny was right."

"What about now?"

"Making love is far better than talking about mushrooms with you."

He started to laugh at her statement and had to grab a pillow to muffle his mirth when he couldn't stop.

Jessica shifted, climbing over him, caged him with her arms and legs and wrenched the pillow from his grip. "Oh, you think talking about mushrooms with me is funny now, do you?"

He dragged one finger from her chin to the tip of her breast, relishing her small gasp as her sensitive nipple pebbled. "I do."

Jessica pushed her breast harder against his hand. "I love our silly nonsense."

"So do I. But this is not nonsense." He drew

a circle around the fullness of her breast. "We could still have a lot of fun in bed together even when we're an old married couple."

"Samuel mentioned that."

He grasped her waist and moved her so she was sitting over his hips. "What else did your other instructors mention about making love?"

"That making love once will never be enough for me. I am a Westfall, and we are a passionate people."

He cupped her sweet derriere in his hands and squeezed. "Then I'm the most fortunate of men to have been well and truly captivated."

He tumbled her onto the mattress and turned her under him, eager to discover how adventurous in bed she might turn out to be. She seemed in no hurry to leave his bed, so he decided to make the most of his good fortune. As her legs wrapped around his hips and her hands slid down his back to his own rear, he shuddered in her grip.

"I'm so grateful you chose me, Jessica," he whispered. "If you hadn't demanded a kiss, I might never know I could be this happy."

For an answer, Jessica dragged him down for more kisses that lasted until dawn lightened the room.

Chapter Eighteen

———— • ————

Jessica tapped on the Stapleton study's open door a little after nine the next morning and let herself in. Her father's summons had brought her rushing downstairs as quickly as she could make herself presentable, hoping to hear Father was at last ready to be reasonable about Giddy. "You wanted to see me, Father?"

"Yes, come in. Come in."

He waved her in urgently. Her father's face was grave, and she was instantly on her guard when he shut the door behind her. "What's the matter?"

"Sit down."

He came back to a chair and waited until she complied, but his tone kept Jessica in a panic. Did he know she'd been with Gideon last night?

"I have had a great many interesting conversations about you in recent days," he began.

She swallowed. "Oh?"

"Lord Newfield spoke to me about arranging a marriage between you and his son early last night. He indicated that you would be gratified to be his son's wife."

"No! I don't like Lord James at all," she cried. "What did you say to him?"

"I told Newfield that I would not consider his son's request until he came to see me himself."

"Lord James left last night. We think he's gone to propose to Lady Hannah Alexander at last."

"His father does not know that." Father pursed his lips, and then tapped on the arm of his chair. "Do you want to hear about another conversation concerning you?"

What could be worse than Lord Newfield claiming she'd want to be a fortune hunter's wife? "Yes, Father."

"Whitfield asked permission to court you two days ago. I said no, of course, even though he confessed he had kissed you. A lesson, he said it was. There will be no more lessons."

They were way beyond mere lessons in kissing now although she'd never admit it. She tried not to blush harder as she thought of last night and Gideon's large hands holding her close against his bare skin.

Jessica knew who she was meant to marry.

She could not wait to call Quigley Hill home and Gideon her husband.

"Do you understand my dilemma? I have two bachelors interested in claiming your hand in marriage in the space of a week. One I discovered would use any means, even offering to buy Quigley Hill with your dowry, to gain my approval."

"What?" she shrieked.

"Whitfield refused the sale," her father promised. "But then in the next breath announced his interest in you, too. Very suspicious timing. I can only imagine you appealed to Gideon for help in thwarting Lord James and to make it appear Lord James had competition."

She stared at him in shock. "I did no such thing," she confessed. "Was that why you refused Giddy a chance to court me? You think I would stoop so low as to put him up to it?"

"Whitfield was considered a trusted friend until this week, now I am not so sure I know him at all. How many men can be persuaded to set aside long-held beliefs and upend their life in the space of a week?"

She gaped and sat forward. "You would deny Whitfield your friendship because *I* kissed *him*."

"You defend him?"

"I love him," she whispered. "I love Gideon."

"Oh, you love him now do you?" Her father's brows shot up. "You've managed to twist him around your fingers since you were a child. I did not wish to believe your sister's accusations of a flirtation, but I believe her now. She would not lie about something so important as your future, and I saw you together in the music room. To think I trusted you both implicitly."

"You were right to trust him." Jessica lifted her chin. "He's been a good friend to me, and a confidant. I never hid from you that I liked him. But my feelings have changed. I'm not a little girl who can be content with him ruffling my hair anymore. I *do* love him! I hated being in London because he was not there with me."

Father lifted a finger, and then his head tilted a little to one side. He squinted at her, and she hoped he was finally understanding the truth behind her words.

Suddenly his expression grew even darker. "I would have preferred not to be the last to know that your respect went deeper before everyone else did. Why didn't you say something sooner?"

"It was a very sudden realization, made without discussing the matter with anyone. I never imagined you would object that I loved Giddy."

Father sighed and looked away first. "From

now on, you will always be in the company of a suitable chaperone when he is around. There will be no more whispered conversations together, no more duets. You will remain in this house and in our company until I make my decision about your future, young lady."

That didn't seem so bad. Jessica had wanted to remain in the country. Closer to Giddy was preferable to not having any chance at seeing him. Gideon had suggested patience, and while not usually her habit, she would try to be very patient for their sake. "Yes, Father."

Jessica jumped as the door to Father's study rattled loudly with the force of a knock. She spun about in her chair, hoping Gideon had come to ask for her hand in marriage again.

"One moment," Father called. He came around the desk. "I have known Whitfield for years, and just the other day he swore to remain a bachelor all his life. You heard him yourself."

Jessica blushed. "It is not so strange. People change their minds and their hearts all the time. You did."

Father slumped against the desk. "Indeed, but I was never opposed to marriage the way he had been."

"I know."

Her father frowned. "I insist you behave yourself."

The knock came again on Father's study

door, startling them both to turn around, and she heard Lord Newfield call out impatiently. Father looked at her. "Do you know for a fact Lord James went back to London?"

"No, but that is where Lady Hannah usually resides."

Father stared at the door as another knock came. "Damn rude fellow. I think I will send the father toward Cornwell instead."

Father kissed her on the top of her head. "Return to your room, and we will talk again later. When Lord Newfield learns that his son has fled without proposing to you, I expect he will be quite surly."

"I'm going," she promised before she fled upstairs via the connecting library door.

———— ◆ ————

Gideon glared at his tardy servants. "About time," he snapped.

"Sorry, sir. I had to finish putting on a pot of stew for your supper," Mrs. Mills admonished.

"I was just about done tallying up the housekeeping accounts," Mrs. Harrow protested. "I always do it on Saturdays."

He turned his attention to Mr. Lewis and raised one brow. "Well?"

The fellow shrugged. "Didn't know it would

be this urgent."

"Well, now you do." Gideon turned away. They were not to blame for his mood but their responses were not helping improve it. "I want the room across the hall cleared out completely today."

"But sir, it were your mother's room," Mrs. Harrow cried out.

"And it will be my wife's next."

He wanted the work to start on clearing out his mother's old sitting room today so that Jessica could arrange everything as she liked it, when her father finally approved him to be a husband.

Everything in there was covered in dust cloths, except for his mother's old pianoforte, which he'd been practicing on. That was not good enough.

He turned around when his staff said not a word more.

Mrs. Harrow's cheeks had turned pink, and Mrs. Mills had become pale. Mr. Lewis folded his arms over his chest and his stare was decidedly belligerent.

Lewis spoke first. "When?"

"When what?"

"When are you getting dragged to the altar?"

"I don't know," he confessed.

Mrs. Harrow took a pace forward, her smile was tentative. "Who are you going to marry, dearie?"

He smiled. "Lady Jessica, if her father lets me," he told them, and then waited for them to point out his unsuitability.

The ladies shrieked and rushed to hug him. Since they never did that, or hadn't since he'd been a boy, he found himself the shocked recipient of their boundless enthusiasm.

"Oh, sir!"

"Oh, my!"

He squinted down at them. He'd never known them to be rendered that speechless ever before. "I assume by that you don't actually object?"

"Oh, indeed we do not, sir! She's long been our favorite, hasn't she?"

"Indeed, sir. She'll be a breath of fresh air about the place."

He snorted back a laugh. "I thought so, too."

Mrs. Harrow held out her arms suddenly. "But, sir. We should not be clearing out your mother's room without Lady Jessica if this will be her home soon."

"I don't know about soon." He looked at the women in consternation. "But everything in there is covered in dust and I think I saw a cobweb at the cornice."

"We'll freshen up the room for you, dust and clean everything before she visits us next. When might that be?"

He sighed. "I've no idea."

"But you will be seeing her today?"

"No. I am banished from Stapleton for the present."

"You shouldn't let his lordship stop you seeing her," Lewis suggested, scratching his chin. "If you want her for your wife, you'd better not take no for an answer this time."

Gideon scowled. He couldn't think of a reasonable excuse to visit and he'd been racking his brain all morning.

Mrs. Harrow wrung her hands. "I can't fathom why his grace wouldn't approve of you for his daughter. She's always favored you."

"Perhaps my age is a factor."

"You're a young man," Mrs. Harrow exclaimed.

He smiled at Mrs. Harrow's foolishness. "Counting the years, I'm five and thirty, not eight, you know."

"You act young," Mrs. Mills insisted. "But we are all looking forward to your next birthday, and now we'll have Lady Jessica to plan a special party for you."

"She does put great stock in celebrating everything." He smiled. "I'm sure she'll like that very much."

"I'll ready the carriage," Lewis decided. He looked Gideon over. "Perhaps you should change. She should have flowers, too. I'll pick her favorites for you to take to her."

Gideon gaped as Lewis rushed from the house. How the devil did his man know which flowers Jessica liked best?

"We've so much to do before the happy day arrives!" Mrs. Harrow said. "We'll need to air all the rooms, polish the best silver in the house in preparation for the wedding."

"His grace will host the breakfast, but I'm sure you newlyweds will host a dinner or two afterward," Mrs. Mills suggested. "I'll help by checking on the contents of the wine cellar and polishing the glassware. She likes sherry at dinner, doesn't she?"

He nodded slowly. "I'll leave you to it then."

"That would be best." The ladies urged him toward the staircase. "Off you go, dearie, and change into clothes better suited to courting. When you see her, do give Lady Jessica our warmest regards."

He headed upstairs to his bedchamber to change in a bit of a daze but glanced at the bed as he passed it.

Gideon could not retreat now. Not when he and Jessica had made love last night. He'd enjoyed her too much, and Jessica had enjoyed him thoroughly, he was sure.

In a sense, he was as much a scoundrel as Lord James might seem to be.

Gideon dressed with particular care, wearing a blue waistcoat beneath his dark suit because

Jessica had mentioned many times that she liked him in blue, and then headed downstairs to see if the carriage was ready.

Mr. Lewis had the gig ready on the drive, Mrs. Mills and Harrow whispering to him. The man whistled, and then grinned at Gideon.

Gideon strode to him. "Did you pick flowers?"

"Aye, I did indeed. On the front bench waiting."

He glanced inside, eyeing the huge bunch Lewis had picked with delight. The man did know Jessica's favorites. Daisy, rose, and lavender. He tugged on his gloves and settled his hat more firmly on his head. He gathered the reins and climbed into the gig.

Mr. Lewis kept hold of the horse's head, and his grin grew sly. "If I may say so, sir, you've made a wise choice. Lady Jessica is the only one for you."

"I agree." He bid Lewis goodbye quickly. But as he drove toward Stapleton Manor, it occurred to him that the only time Lewis smiled lately was when Jessica was mentioned. And he scowled a whole lot more when Mrs. Beck was around. In fact, Lewis' surliness had begun at the beginning of the month, soon after he'd been introduced to Mrs. Beck at the late Mr. Grieves' funeral. He glanced over his shoulder. "Well, I'll be damned. The old fellow must have been worried I'd marry the wrong woman."

He slapped the reins over the horse's rump again and set off smartly for Stapleton Manor. Usually, he would walk the short distance, but he did not believe he had the right to come and go on foot anymore.

He slowed the carriage through the turn of the circular drive and was met by Mr. Brown and a groom at the stairs.

"Good to see you again, Mr. Whitfield," the butler called, grinning as if his face would split open.

"Hello, Brown." He kept his response subdued but his anticipation was growing. It was impossible to keep secrets in a household this size. Brown most likely already knew he was interested in marrying Jessica. Gideon thought he might be happy about it; otherwise the old fellow would have acted far less friendly. "How is the family today?"

"Fine. Fine. Lord Newfield departed an hour ago."

"Ah," he said, delighted to hear the pair had been driven off. "That's a shame."

Brown urged him to the door. "The duchess is expecting you," he explained.

"The duchess? I see. Of course." He frowned though. His call was unplanned. The duke's wife had not been privy to any of his conversations with her husband. With her health so delicate, they'd barely spoken this past week. Stapleton surely would have told her of Gideon's request by now. No doubt she must be disappointed in him. He'd actually promised to keep a distance from Jessica last Christmas, even if, at the time, he'd not been a suitor. It must seem as if he'd broken that promise as soon as Jessica had returned from London unmarried. Most likely he was about to be scolded.

Brown led him to a room he'd rarely spent any time in, a somewhat cramped, intimate chamber beyond the opulence of the white drawing room. The room was bathed in soft light, filled with pillows and comfortable padded chairs. It seemed the new duchess had chosen her own parlor for comfort rather than to make an impression on those who called upon her.

He bowed deeply to her but kept his bunch of flowers for Jessica hidden behind his back.

The duchess was alone, a piece of needlework in her hands. She studied him a few long and painful moments then patted the cushion beside her. "Come sit by me, Gideon."

He took a deep breath and crossed the room. "Thank you."

She smiled when she noticed the flowers in his hand. "What am I going to do with you?"

He frowned and put the flowers aside. "I know you must be very cross with me. I am sure—"

"My dear man. Do you think I'm angry with you?"

He looked at her sharply. "You're not?"

"Of course I am not." She leaned close. "I also know Jessica did not suddenly decide to kiss you because she wanted to convince Lord James he had competition. Do not forget, I know my daughter very well now."

His heart raced, but he kept quiet.

"Lord Newfield left in a snit this morning, and we are all very glad to see the back of him. I am grateful for the distraction your courtship with Jessica has afforded my husband."

"I am not allowed to court Jessica."

"So says the duke now, but let us not lie about this to each other. You are quite obviously engaged in a courtship behind his back." She shook her head. "I saw her devastated expression when her father refused to invite you for dinner tonight."

"I couldn't stay away." He gulped. "Jessica knows how I feel about her. I will not abandon the chase as the duke clearly expects me to."

"I do not think Jessica will be easily persuaded away from you, either, sir." The duchess laughed. "As we both know, Jessica has a mind of her own. She adores you. She always has."

"We both know there are other considerations. Jessica deserves so much more than to marry a mere gentleman of modest means."

The duchess made a sound of discontent. "When it is eventually announced that you are to marry, the size of your fortune and lack of title will not be important. When the family sees her smile at you, and you at her, they will believe it is a love match and be happy for the both of you. But until that day comes, it is important that everyone believes Jessica's reputation is above reproach."

"I would never do anything—" he began, but the duchess held up her hand.

"It was never you I worried about. I know your heart, Gideon Whitfield. I have known your feelings for Jessica existed for a long time. Jessica, however, can at times be impetuous and often acts without thinking of the consequences of her adventures." She sighed. "All I am asking is that you continue to protect her to the best of your ability."

"I always will," he promised.

"Good. Now, you will find Jessica in the drawing room with Mrs. Warner. According to my husband's wishes, you must be chaperoned at all times, and I apologize for that unnecessary obstacle in your courtship. My husband has always been overprotective of his youngest daughter, as you must already have seen," she said. "Jessica will not tolerate his coddling for long. She can never bear to be cooped up inside. You have no idea of her unhappiness in London."

"Some. Jessica does love the freedom to come and go. But…" Gideon wet his lips. "I must say it is a great relief to know you support the match and don't wish to throw a flowerpot at me."

"There's still time." The duchess smiled, and he realized she was only teasing him. "How could I think to harm you when Jessica has been floating about the place almost from the moment she saw you again? You make her so very happy, and that is all I want for her."

"Thank you."

The duchess gestured toward the door. "Now off you go. Do not be put off by my husband's abrupt manner. He is ever slow to change."

Gideon bowed. "I'll do my best to convince the duke of the benefits as soon as I can." He collected his bunch of flowers and strode off toward the drawing room.

Gideon stepped into the chamber—and his breath caught. My God, he was nearly betrothed to the most beautiful creature in existence. Not even Mrs. Warner's scowling presence could dim his heart's wild clatter.

Jessica wore a pretty blue gown, hair swept up into an elegant arrangement. But it was her smile of welcome that drew him across the room. "Good afternoon, Lady Jessica. Mrs. Warner."

Jessica curtsied, and he bowed and then handed her the flowers.

"Mr. Whitfield. These are lovely." When Jessica's gaze lifted, the look in her eyes was most definitely lusty.

Chapter Nineteen

———•———

Gideon caught Jessica's hand in his. "I'm glad you like them."

"They're perfect, just like you," Jessica whispered.

"Oh please, just kiss the girl before she swoons," Rebecca grumbled.

"Swooning?" Gideon asked, taking in Jessica's appearance. Her breathing seemed to be very quick and her cheeks were slowly turning pink.

Jessica leaned closer to him to whisper, "How does anyone live with this feeling?"

"Are you all right?" Gideon whispered.

"Never better," she whispered back. "I just can't forget last night."

"Neither can I."

Mrs. Warner plucked the flowers from Jessica's hands. "I'll have these put into a vase.

Father is being ridiculous about this."

"Thank you," Jessica called when her sister strode out of the room. "That was very considerate of her to give us some privacy."

"Yes, quite surprising really." Jessica drew even closer but he frowned. "We'd better behave, though."

"For now," she agreed.

Gideon took Jessica's elbow in his palm and steered her toward the window seat. "She makes a terrible chaperone. Your father will not be pleased when he finds out she left us."

"Oh, I think she's perfect. Besides, she knows you love me."

"Indeed." He cupped Jessica's face. "More than I ever thought I could love anyone. But I've taken more risks with your reputation than I ever intended."

"No more than I have done myself. I asked you to kiss me, and I want more," she whispered. She inched closer. "I've always hated waiting to see you. You should have come to London with us."

"You were busy," he reminded her.

"Meeting unsuitable men. Fortune hunters." She peered out toward the door and moved another inch in his direction.

Gideon clenched his hands together between his knees. They shouldn't be alone, but there were things he needed to tell Jessica about his life that required this very privacy. "What is your earliest memory of me?"

"I don't know." She frowned, looking down at her hands. "Holding your hand, I suppose. Mine was tiny then."

He reached for hers now, sliding her palm over his. There was still a considerable disparity between them despite her growing up. There always would be. "I have been your father's friend for a long time, but I was your brother's friend first. Do you recall that?"

She clenched his hand tightly. "You haven't stayed friends with them. Did you argue?"

"No. They always belonged to a younger crowd. We drifted apart as many men do." He smiled quickly. "My first memory of you was a few months after your birth. After your mother died. I came to visit, and heard you crying in the nursery. The house was in something of an uproar at that time, and I thought your family might be with you, so I went upstairs into the nursery. Your sisters were there, Fanny and Rebecca. They were squabbling over the top of your cot, and you were just sitting there sobbing."

"I've never heard this story before."

She looked so worried, he hastened to reassure her. "It ends well. The servants were nowhere to be seen, so I picked you up and you stopped crying. I remember it was very sudden, and you clung to me and would not be put back down. So I kept you in my arms to keep you happy. Fanny and Rebecca flounced off in a huff, and I went to find the duke with you.

"Your father hadn't been coping well with the loss of your mother, I realized, but he was your father and responsible for you. So I took him to task for letting you cry for so long. I was quite angry back then. I thought all fathers were cruel, selfish creatures."

Jessica stared at him. "What did he do?"

"Nothing I expected. You had fallen asleep in my arms, actually, while I was busy berating him. You didn't know me, but somehow you trusted me from the first, and Stapleton couldn't stop staring at us. His silence annoyed me, and I threw out a few more choice accusations about neglect, drunkenness, and warned him that if he didn't start being your father, I would take you home and look after you myself. That got his attention. He ordered me to stay where I was. I had you in my arms still, and once my initial fury abated, I waited, trembling, for the duke to return to whip me for my impertinence."

"Father would never whip anyone," she promised.

"Well, I did not know that about him at the time. *My* father had for less, so I figured holding on to you for as long as possible was the only way to delay a beating I deserved."

"No one deserves such treatment," Jessica whispered.

"When the duke returned nearly an hour later, your sisters had been banished to separate rooms for the next week, a few staff had been given their marching orders and the duke, more sensible than he'd been perhaps in months, promised he would quit drinking that very day. He asked for you back and swore to me that he'd never neglect you again."

"That is so sweet."

"It was a very long time ago. Your father started inviting me to dinner after that, mainly I think so I wouldn't be by myself. Jess, I have watched over you from a distance for so long, it has become a habit. I let you tell me your secrets and kept them, even from him, but I could never tell you mine. You were too young."

She seemed shocked by that. "What secrets could you possibly have that I couldn't already know about?"

"My father beat me when I was a boy. Usually for no good reason. He hurt my mother, too. I was sixteen when I hit him back."

"Good." Her expression changed to one of annoyance. "Is it because of him you never trusted yourself to love anyone?"

"I broke his nose and his arm in that fight, Jessica. I lost my temper completely but he never hit me again, or hurt my mother until the day she died."

"I'm glad."

He frowned at her. "You don't seem surprised."

"I'm not really. I saw his portrait when I was young, and he frightened me. I've since heard a few things to confirm that my feeling about him were right. He was a cold man, cruel, but you're not like him. You'd hurt yourself before you ever hurt your wife or your children."

"There are no guarantees I won't turn out just like him."

"That's a risk anyone who really loved you would be happy to make." She lay her head against his shoulder. "Didn't we decide the other night that we are a team, Giddy? We want the same things."

"A quiet life in the country and dinner conversation about fungus?"

Jessica sighed. "What could be better!"

He grinned. She did make him happy. She made him imagine a great future might be theirs if he was willing to set aside his fears. Jessica would know his character better than anyone, too.

He kissed the top of her head. "My angel, my torment, my heart."

Unfortunately, the Duke of Stapleton chose that moment to stomp into the room.

He looked twice when he saw Gideon, and

284 | HEATHER BOYD

his eyes narrowed even farther when he spied
Jessica cuddling up to him. The duke gathered
himself up, but then lost his temper enough to
shout, "What did I say about you being alone
with him?"

Not to be outdone, Jessica set her lips into a
mulish line as she sat up. "You and Gillian were
alone every night before you ever dreamed of
asking her to marry you."

"Gillian was a widow. You are an innocent."

Not quite so innocent anymore, and that
was his fault for not doing things the right way
from the beginning.

Jessica giggled. "He's not going to ravish me
in your drawing room!"

Gideon patted her hand before she got
carried away in her defense of him and blurted
out the truth. He certainly wouldn't ravish her
here, in her father's home. He'd rather wait
until they were at Quigley Hill again, where
they could take their time. She would look very
fine, naked and panting, spread over his leather
settee or dining table, where he might feast
upon her. "We can talk another time."

"You mean when it fits with his grace's
schedule? No, I'm not going to wait another
day and have him banish you all over again. He
has to start sharing you; otherwise, I'll be an old
maid by the time he lets me have you!" Jessica
kissed Gideon full on the lips. "It is *my* turn to

convince him, Giddy."

"Don't go too far with this," he warned, but he couldn't hold back a smile. She really was something when she got worked up into a temper.

"I'll go as far as I need to have you," she warned.

She faced her father, and not for the first time did Gideon feel sorry that the duke was standing in her way. After eighteen years of Jessica managing her family, it was surprising the duke had the fortitude left to resist even this long.

"You are not being reasonable," she told the duke.

"Do not talk back to me, daughter. I will lock you in your room if you don't behave," her father threatened.

"I thought you might say that." She turned sad eyes on her father, and her bottom lip trembled. "Don't you want me to be happy?"

"Of course I do." But the duke suddenly sounded far less sure of himself.

Jessica turned to Gideon, and he saw tears in her eyes. Fake ones, he decided. "I'm going to be locked up, Giddy, and made very unhappy."

Thank heavens he'd learned to understand her tricks years ago. "I expect so."

"Will you elope with me?"

Gideon stood and tugged down his waistcoat. "We talked about this. I'd rather not start our marriage with a scandal."

She leaned against him, worming her way into his arms, ignoring her father's spluttering. "We may have no choice. I love you too much to let you go without a fight."

Gideon brushed his fingers down her cheek. "I love you, too, but if he says we cannot marry, we will not."

"Well, I'm in favor of creating a scandal," she announced, and then flounced toward the door. "I'm going to pack," she called at the top of her voice.

Gideon pinched the bridge of his nose. Every servant in Stapleton Manor should have heard that remark, or will have by nightfall.

The duke gaped after her. "Pack?"

"I swear I'm not taking her away from you," Gideon promised as he sat down again.

When he looked up, Stapleton was scowling at him. "I've had it wrong all along, haven't I? It's not Jessica who needs protecting." Stapleton's eyes widened. "It's you. From *her*."

"I wouldn't say I need protection," Gideon murmured, but then winced. He didn't mind Jessica's habit of kissing him, but doing so in front of her father wasn't good for Stapleton's temper, obviously. Gideon cleared his throat. "You have to let Jessica go eventually."

The duke brushed his hand over his mouth, his eyes wide. "She did say she kissed you. I didn't want to believe her at first. And then Rebecca warned she'd become secretive and could not be found after dinner. And then she told me this morning that..."

"Told you what?"

But the duke did not answer. He went for the brandy, pouring one glass, drinking it, and then pouring another. He did not offer Gideon one, and stood sipping the second, staring outside.

Gideon loosened his cravat a little, uncertain of what the duke would do and say next.

The duke suddenly moved, pouring brandy into another glass and carrying it over to Gideon. He thrust out the glass. "Drink that. As one newly married man to the next, you'll need to keep your wits about you once you join your name and heart to a Westfall."

He took the offered drink, deciding that was as much of a blessing as he would ever get. "When will the wedding be?"

The duke drained his glass. "A month. I'll have the banns called tomorrow."

Gideon grinned. "Thank you, your grace."

"Don't you dare thank me, don't *your grace* me...or ever consider calling me *Papa*, either. You're stealing my daughter, and she *wants* to be stolen."

"As you prefer," he murmured, finding the

situation funny. "On the bright side, I will not be taking her very far away. I am sure you could still see her every day if you wish. May I see Jessica to tell her the news?"

Although the duke grumbled, he yanked on the bell and had a grinning servant fetch Jessica back. She danced into the room on her toes, right to his side, and kissed his cheek. "Have we convinced him or are we eloping?"

"Not eloping, but your behavior might have decided him in our favor."

She turned away. "I really do want to marry him."

Her father sighed. "Did you actually intend eloping if you couldn't marry him?"

"I mentioned it was an option but Giddy, of course, refused immediately," Jessica said, wincing. "He's too proper for that, and he knew I'd want my family at our wedding. He's been quite sensible and accommodating of all my requests so far. I think he will make an admirable husband, and a son-in-law to you."

Her father raised his face to the heavens. "I'm not sure I'll have the strength to do this again."

Jessica laughed. "Poor Papa."

Gideon tapped Jessica's shoulder, bringing her attention back to him. When their eyes met, he felt a certainty about his place in the world, and at Jessica's side. Gideon wouldn't come between father and daughter. He didn't have to, he already had found his place, though there was one thing left to say to make his decision to marry absolutely official.

He dropped to one knee there and then and took her tiny hand in his. "Lady Jessica Westfall. I would be honored for all the days of my life if you would accept my suit and consider me for your husband."

The duke made an inarticulate sound and turned his back.

Jessica smiled down at him, tears shining in her eyes. "I thought you'd never ask."

"There couldn't be anyone but you."

"I know. I would never allow anyone to come between us." Jessica beamed and made to pull him up. "Of course I'm going to marry you. We belong together."

Gideon rose to his feet quickly. He caressed her cheek, wiped away the tears that clung to her lashes, and then produced a ring from his pocket that held a small sapphire. He slipped it on her slender finger, finding it a perfect fit. "Darling, Jess."

"This was your mother's ring?"

He nodded. "She would have loved you."

They kissed to seal their vow to each other, Jessica's hand clutched in his.

They drew back when the noise of the duke clearing his throat grew so loud it was distracting.

"All right!" the duke grumbled, wiping his face with a handkerchief.

Jessica looked at him in astonishment. "Were you crying too, Papa?"

"Of course not. Damn dusty in here," Stapleton grumbled, and made a show of blowing his nose. "Have to speak to the housekeeper about it."

Gideon hid a grin. He wasn't deceived one bit. "Then what did you mean by your outburst?"

"I'll arrange for a special license so you can marry sooner, just stop doing that while I'm in the room."

Jessica wrapped Gideon's arms around her. "You proposed to Gillian in front of a witness. Mrs. Hawthorne said you were terribly romantic. What is so wrong about being affectionate with the one you love?"

Too many things to name right now. Her father may have approved the marriage, but it might be a long time before he was comfortable with it. "Are you sure you should be baiting him still?"

"Quite sure." Jessica grinned. "I ignored quite a bit because I saw how happy Gillian made him when they were together."

"We encouraged them, love," Gideon whispered in her ear, making her shiver. "There is a difference."

"I knew I should have kept you two apart

after last winter," the duke grumbled again. "How long has this thing been going on under my nose?"

Gideon straightened. He couldn't remember a time when Jessica's happiness hadn't meant more to him than his own. There was no date when he'd *fallen* in love with her. He just was. "I should like to start lying to you now, if you don't mind."

Jessica giggled when her father gaped. She kissed Gideon one more time before she rushed from the room, saying, "I have to tell Gillian and Rebecca the happy news!"

There was a vast silence after her departure then the duke turned to him. "What other requests has my daughter made of you," he demanded, glass half raised to his lips.

"I think the less you know, the easier you'll sleep at night," Gideon murmured.

When the duke opened his mouth and closed it again, Gideon took a sip of his drink. The poor man seemed to be reeling still. In time, he'd accept his daughter had grown up. Jessica had grown into a bold and passionate woman. He liked everything about her. He was looking forward to the future in a way he never had before.

The duke cleared his throat and Gideon glanced his way again. The duke was grinning widely and then winked. "Forgive me. Refusing you was the hardest thing I've ever done. I had to be sure."

Gideon's brows lifted. "You were testing me?"

The duke nodded. "Her resolve more than yours. We've only been back a week and you had both seemed disinclined to tie the knot until now. But you were right about her all along. When she made up her mind about a husband, she didn't waste any time claiming you for herself and quite vocally, too."

Gideon grinned. "She had the talk from seven different people, you know. So many bad ideas put into her head," he warned.

"I see." The duke dug his finger under his cravat and tugged. "You know, if we are going to remain on good terms, you *will* have to lie to me. There is only so much I need to know about your relationship with my daughter. Welcome to the family."

"Thank you." Gideon hid a grin as he added, "Father."

The duke's shocked expression was utterly priceless. "Not *that*, either. You can address me as you've always done. Nicolas will do when we are alone."

And that was fine with Gideon.

———•———

If you enjoyed the story don't miss the rest of
the Saints and Sinners series...

The Duke and I

The Duke of Stapleton abhors Christmas nonsense,
but could a kiss exchanged under mistletoe with his
daughter's shy companion alter his opinion of the
season?

An Earl of Her Own

Rebecca Warner has no time for the maddening
Lord Rafferty. Until the earl proves her most ardent
ally—both in and out of his bedchamber.

The Lady Tamed

A lady possessed of a fortune. A poor actor with a
shady past. It's the role of a lifetime...but their
contract said nothing about falling in love.

More Regency Romance from
Heather Boyd...

———•———

And many more

About Heather Boyd

———◆———

USA Today Bestselling Author Heather Boyd believes every character she creates deserves their own happily-ever-after—no matter how much trouble she puts them through. With that goal in mind, she writes steamy romances that skirt the boundaries of propriety to keep readers enthralled until the wee hours of the morning. Heather has published over 40 regency romance novels and shorter works full of daring seductions and distinguished rogues. She lives north of Sydney, Australia, with her trio of rogues and pair of four-legged overlords.

You can find details of her writing at
www.Heather-Boyd.com

Printed in February 2023
by Rotomail Italia S.p.A., Vignate (MI) - Italy